Underground Man

By
Gabriel De Tarde

Underground Man
by Gabriel De Tarde

Copyright © 2023

All Rights reserved.
No part of this publication may be reproduced, stored in a retrieval system, or transmitted in any form or by any means, electronic, mechanical, photocopying or Otherwise, without the written permission of the publisher.

The author/editor asserts the moral right to be identified as the author/editor of this work.

ISBN: 978-93-57279-58-1

Published by
DOUBLE 9 BOOKS
2/13-B, Ansari Road
Daryaganj, New Delhi – 110002
info@double9books.com
www.double9books.com
Tel. 011-40042856

This book is under public domain

ABOUT THE AUTHOR

Gabriel Tarde was a French sociologist, criminologist, and social psychologist (born 12 March 1843; died 13 May 1904). He believed that little psychological exchanges between people are the foundation of sociology.

He was hired as a contemporary philosophy professor at the Collège de France in 1900. He was therefore the most well-known contemporary opponent of Durkheim's sociology. He corresponded with members of the newly established criminal anthropology in the 1880s, particularly Enrico Ferri and Cesare Lombroso. Tarde eventually rose to prominence as the top criminologist from a "French school."

Among the ideas, Tarde pioneered were the collective mind (which Gustave Le Bon picked up and refined) and economic psychology, where he foresaw a lot of contemporary trends. Émile Durkheim's work received harsh criticism from Tarde at both the methodological and theoretical levels. Durkeim and his disciples scorned and immediately disregarded his ideas as "metaphysics," and they went on to mainly create sociology as a "science."

He criticized Cesare Lombroso's formulation of the atavistic criminal theory. As part of a larger process of repetition compulsion, Tarde underlined the criminal's propensity to go back to the scene of the crime and repeat it. He emphasized the value of the creative role model in society and claimed that "genius is the power to generate one's own children."

CONTENTS

PREFACE 7
INTRODUCTORY 14
I.
    PROSPERITY 15
II.
    THE CATASTROPHE 24
III.
    THE STRUGGLE 29
IV.
    SAVED! 40
V.
    REGENERATION 45
VI.
    LOVE 56
VII.
    THE ÆSTHETIC LIFE 62

PREFACE

It reflects not at all on Mr Cloudesley Brereton's admirable work of translation to remark how subtly the spirit of such work as this of M. Tarde's changes in such a process. There are certain things peculiar, I suppose, to every language in the world, certain distinctive possibilities in each. To French far more than to English, belong the intellectual liveliness, the cheerful, ironical note, the professorial playfulness of this present work. English is a less nimble, more various and moodier tongue, not only in the sound and form of its sentences but in its forms of thought. It clots and coagulates, it proliferates and darkens, one jests in it with difficulty and great danger to a sober reputation, and one attempts in vain to figure Professor Giddings and Mr Benjamin Kidd, Doctor Beattie Crozier and Mr Wordsworth Donisthorpe glittering out into any so cheerful an exploit as this before us. Like Mr Gilbert's elderly naval man, they "never larks nor plays", and if indeed they did so far triumph over the turgid intricacies of our speech and the conscientious gravity of our style of thought, there would still be the English public to consider, a public easily offended by any lack of straightforwardness in its humorists, preferring to be amused by known and recognised specialists in that line, in relation to themes of recognised humorous tendency, and requiring in its professors as the concomitant of a certain dignified inaccessibility of thought and language, an honourable abstinence from the treacheries, as it would consider them, of irony and satire. Imagine a Story of the Future from Mr Herbert Spencer! America and the north of England would have swept him out of all respect.... But M. Tarde being not only a Member of the Institute and Professor at the College of France, but a Frenchman, was free to give these fancies that entertained him, public, literary, and witty expression, without self-destruction, and produce what has, in its English dress, a curiously unfamiliar effect. Yet the English reader who can overcome his natural disinclination to this union of intelligence and jesting will find a vast amount of suggestion in M. Tarde's fantastic abundance, and bringing his habitual gravity to bear may even succeed in digesting off the humour altogether, and emerging with edification of—it must be admitted—a rather miscellaneous sort.

It is perhaps remarkable that for so many people, so tremendous a theme as the material future of mankind should only be approachable either through a method of conscientiously technical, pseudo-scientific discussion that is in effect scarcely an approach at all or else in this mood of levity. I know of no book in this direction that can claim to be a permanent success which combines a tolerable intelligibility with a simple good faith in the reader. One may speculate how this comes about? The subject it would seem is so grave and great as to be incompatibly out of proportion to the affairs and conditions of the individual life about which our workaday thinking goes on. We are interested indeed, but at the same time we feel it is outside us and beyond us. To turn one's attention to it is at once to get an effect of presumption, strain, and extravagant absurdity. It is like picking up a spade to attack a mountain, and one's instinct is to put oneself right in the eyes of one's fellow-men at once, by a few unmistakably facetious flourishes. It is the same instinct really as that protective "foolery" in which schoolboys indulge when they embark upon some hopeless undertaking, or find themselves entirely outclassed at a game.

The same instinct one finds in the facetious "parley vous Francey" of a low class Englishman who would in secret like very much to speak French, but in practice only admits such an idea as a laughable absurdity. To give a concrete form to your sociological speculations is to strip them of all their poor pretensions, and leave them shivering in palpable inadequacy. It is not because the question is unimportant, but because it is so overwhelmingly important that this jesting about the Future, this fantastic and "ironical" fiction goes on. It is the only medium to express the vague, ill-formed, new ideas with which we are all labouring. It does not give any measure of our real sense of the proportion of things that the Future should appear in our literature as a sort of comic rally and harlequinade after the serious drama of the Present—in which the heroes and heroines of the latter turn up again in novel and undignified positions; but it seems to be the only method at present available by which we may talk about our race's material Destiny at all.

M. Tarde, in this special case before us, pursues a course of elusive ironies; sometimes he jests at contemporary ideas by imagining them in burlesque realisation, sometimes he jests at contemporary facts by transposing them into strange surroundings, sometimes he broaches fancies of his own chiefly for their own sake, yet with the well-managed literary equivalent of the palliating laugh of conversational diffidence. It is interesting to remark upon the clearness, the French reasonableness and order of his conceptions throughout. He thinks, as the French seem always to think, in terms of a humanity at once more lucid and more limited than the mankind with which we English have to deal. There are no lapses, no fogs and mysteries, no total inadequacies, no brutalities and left-handedness—and no dark gleams of the divinity, about these amused bright people of five hundred years ahead, who are overtaken by the great solar catastrophe. They have established a world state and eliminated the ugly and feeble. You imagine the gentlemen in that Utopia moving gracefully—with beautifully trimmed nails and beards—about the most elegant and ravishing of ladies, their charm greatly enhanced by the *pince-nez*, that is in universal wear. They all speak not Esperanto—but Greek, which strikes one as a little out of the picture—and all being more or less wealthy and pretty women and handsome men, "as common as blackberries" and as available, "human desire rushed with all its might towards the only field that remained open to it",—politics. From that it was presently turned back again by a certain philosophical financier, who, most delightfully, secured his work for ever, as the reader may learn in detail, by erecting a statue of Louis Philippe in wrought aluminium against any return of the flood—and then what remained? The most brilliant efflorescence of poetry and art!

One does not quite know how far M. Tarde is in this first part of his story jesting at his common countrymen's precisions and finalities and unenterprising, exact arrangements, and how far he is sharing them. Throughout he seems to assume that men can really make finished plans, and carry them out, and settle things for ever, and so assure us this state of elegant promenading among the arts, whereas the whole charm and interest of making plans and carrying out, lies to the more typical kind of Englishman, in his ineradicable, his innate, instinctive conviction, that he will, try as he may, never carry them out at all, but something else adventurously and happily unexpected and different. M. Tarde gives his world the unexpected, but it comes, not insidiously as a unique difference in every individual and item concerned, but from without. Just as Humanity, handsome and charming, has grouped itself pleasantly, rationally, and in the best of taste for ever in its studios, in its *salons*, at its little green tables, at its *tables d'hôte*, in its *cabinets particuliers*—the sun goes out!

In the idea of that solar extinction there are extraordinary imaginative possibilities, and M. Tarde must have exercised considerable restraint to prevent their running away with him and so jarring with the ironical lightness of his earlier passages. The conception of the sun seized in a mysterious, chill grip and flickering from hue to hue in the skies of a darkened, amazed and terrified world, could be presented in images of stupendous majesty and splendour. There arise visions of darkened cities and indistinct, multitudinous, fleeing crowds, of wide country-sides of chill dismay, of beasts silent with the fear of this last eclipse, and bats and night-birds abroad amidst the lost daylight creatures and fluttering perplexed on noiseless wings. Then the abrupt sight of the countless stars made visible by this great abdication, the thickening of the sky to stormy masses of cloud so that these are hidden again, the soughing of a world-wide wind, and then first little flakes and then the drift and driving of the multiplying snow into the dim illumination of lamps, of windows, of street lights lit untimely. Then again, the shiver of the cold, the clutching of hands at coats and wraps, the blind hurrying to shelter and the comfort of a fire—the blaze of fires. One sees the red-lit faces about the fires, sees the furtive glances at the wind-tormented windows, hears the furious knocking of those other strangers barred out, for, "we cannot have everyone in here". The darkness deepens, the cries without die away, and nothing is left but the shift and falling of the incessant snow from roof to ground. Every now and then the disjointed talk would cease altogether, and in the stillness one would hear the faint yet insistent creeping sound of the snowfall. "There is a little food downstairs," one would say. "The servants must not eat it.... We had better lock it upstairs. We may be here—for days." Grim stuff, indeed, one might make of it all, if one dealt with it in realistic fashion, and great and increasing toil one would find to carry on the tale. M. Tarde was well advised to let his hand pass lightly over this episode, to give us a simply pyrotechnic effect of red, yellow, green and pale blue, to let his people flee and die like marionettes beneath the paper snows of a shop window dressed for Christmas, and to emerge after the change with his urbanity unimpaired. His apt jest at the endurance of artists' models, his easy allusion to the hardening effects of fashionable decolletage, is the measure of his dexterous success; his mention of hotel furniture on the terminal moraines of the returning Alpine glaciers, just a happy touch of that flavouring of reality which in abundance would have altogether overwhelmed his purpose.

Directly one thinks at all seriously of such a thing as this solar extinction, one perceives how preposterously hopeless it is to imagine that mankind would make any head against so swift and absolute a fate. Our race would behave just as any single man behaves when death takes him suddenly through some cardiac failure. It would feel very queer, it would want to sit down and alleviate its strange discomfort, it would say something stupid or inarticulate, make an odd gesture or so, and flicker out. But it is compatible with the fantastic and ironical style for M. Tarde to mock our conceit in our race's capacity and pretend men did all sorts of organized and wholesale things quite beyond their capabilities. People flee in "hordes" to Arabia Petræa and the Sahara, and there perform prodigies of resistance. There arises the heroic leader and preserver, Miltiades, who preaches Neo-troglodytism and loves the peerless Lydia, and leads the remnant of humanity underground. So M. Tarde arrives at the idea he is most concerned in developing, the idea of an introverted world, and people following the dwindling heat of the interior, generation after generation, through gallery and tunnel to the core. About that conception he weaves the finest and richest and most suggestive of his fantastic filaments.

Perhaps the best sustained thread in this admirably entertaining tissue is the entire satisfaction of the imaginary historian at the new conditions of life. The earth is made into an interminable honeycomb, all other forms of life than man are eliminated, and our race has developed into a community sustained at a high level of happiness and satisfaction by a constant resort to "social tonics". Half mockingly, half approvingly, M. Tarde here indicates a new conception of human intercourse and criticises with a richly suggestive detachment, the social relationships of to-day. He moves indicatively and lightly over deeps of human possibility; it is in these later passages that our author is essentially found. One may regret he did not further expand his happy opportunity of treating all the social types to-day as ice embedded fossils, his comments on the peasant and artisan are so fine as to provoke the appetite. He rejects the proposition that "society consists in an exchange of services" with the confidence of a man who has thought it finely out. He gives out clearly what so many of us are beginning dimly perhaps to apprehend, that "society consists in the exchange of reflections". The passages subsequent to this pronouncement will be the seed of many interesting developments in any mind sufficiently attuned to his. They constitute the body, the serious reality to which all the rest of this little book is so much dress, adornment and concealment. Very many of us, I believe, are dreaming of the possibility of human groupings based on interest and a common creative impulse rather than on justice and a trade in help and services; and I do not scruple therefore to put my heavy underline and marginal note to M. Tarde's most intimate moment. A page or so further on he is back below his ironical mask again, jesting at the "tribe of sociologists"—the most unsociable of mankind. Thereafter jest, picturesque suggestion, fantasy, philosophical whim, alternate in a continuously delightful fashion to the end—but always with the gleam of a definite intention coming and going within sight of the surface—and one ends at last a half convinced Neo-troglodyte, invaded by a passion of intellectual regret for the varied interests of that inaccessible world and its irradiating love. The description of the development of science, and particularly of troglodytic astronomy, robbed of its material, is a delightful freak of intellectual fantasy, and the philosophical dream of the slow concentration of human life into the final form of a single culminating omniscient, and therefore a completely retrospective and anticipatory being, a being that is, that has cast aside the time garment, is one of these suggestions that have at once something penetratingly plausible, and a sort of colossal and absurd monstrosity. If I may be forgiven a personal intrusion at this point, there is a singular parallelism between this foreshadowed Last Man of M. Tarde's stalactitic philosopher, and a certain *Grand Lunar* I once wrote about in a book called «The First Men in the Moon». And I remember coming upon the same idea in a book by Merejkowski, the title of which I am now totally unable to recall.... But I will not write further on this curiously attractive and deep seated suggestion. My proper business here is, I think, chiefly to direct the reader past the lightness and cheerful superficiality of the opening portions of this book, and its—at the first blush, rather disappointing but critically justifiable, treatment of the actual catastrophe, to these obscure but curiously stimulating and interesting caves, and tunnels, and galleries in which the elusive real thought of M. Tarde lurks—for those who care to follow it up and seize it and understand.

    H. G. WELLS.

INTRODUCTORY

It was towards the end of the twentieth century of the prehistoric era, formerly called the Christian, that took place, as is well known, the unexpected catastrophe with which the present epoch began, that fortunate disaster which compelled the overflowing flood of civilisation to disappear for the benefit of mankind. I have briefly to relate this universal cataclysm and the unhoped-for redemption so rapidly effected within a few centuries of heroic and triumphant efforts. Of course, I shall pass over in silence the particular details which are known to everybody, and shall merely confine myself to the general outlines of the story. But first of all it may be as well to recall in a few words the degree of relative progress already attained by mankind, while still living above ground and on the surface of the earth, on the eve of this momentous event.

I.
PROSPERITY

The zenith of human prosperity seemed to have been reached in the superficial and frivolous sense of the word. For the last fifty years, the final establishment of the great Asiatic-American-European confederacy, and its indisputable supremacy over what was still left, here and there, in Oceania and central Africa of barbarous tribes incapable of assimilation, had habituated all the nations, now converted into provinces, to the delights of universal and henceforth inviolable peace. It had required not less than 150 years of warfare to arrive at this wonderful result. But all these horrors were forgotten. True, there had been many terrific battles between armies of three and four million men, between trains with armour-clad carriages, flung, at full speed, against one another, and opening fire on every side; engagements between squadrons of sub-marines which blew one another up with electric discharges; between fleets of iron-clad balloons, harpooned and ripped up by aerial torpedoes, hurled headlong from the clouds, with thousands of parachutes which violently opened and enveloped each other in a storm of grape-shot as they fell together to earth. Yet of all this warlike mania there only remained a vague poetic remembrance. Forgetfulness is the beginning of happiness, as fear is the beginning of wisdom.

As a solitary exception to the general rule, the nations, after this gigantic blood-letting, did not experience the lethargy that follows from exhaustion, but the calm that the accession of strength produces. The explanation is easy. For about a hundred years the military selection committees had broken with the blind routine of the past and made it a practice to pick out carefully the strongest and best made among the young men, in order to exempt them from the burden of military service which had become purely mechanical, and to send to the depot all the weaklings who were good enough to fulfil the sorely diminished functions of the soldier and even of the non-commissioned officer. That was really a piece of intelligent selection; and the historian cannot conscientiously refuse gratefully to praise this innovation, thanks to which the incomparable beauty of the human race to-day has been gradually developed. In fact, when we now look through the glass cases of our museums of antiquities at those singular collections of caricatures which our ancestors used to call their photographic albums, we can confirm the vastness of the progress thus accomplished, if it is really true that we are actually descended from these dwarfs and scare-crows, as an otherwise trustworthy tradition attests.

From this epoch dates the discovery of the last microbes, which had not yet been analysed by the neo-Pasteurian school. Once the cause of every disease was known, the remedy was not long in becoming known as well, and from that moment, a consumptive or rheumatic patient, or an invalid of any kind became as rare a phenomenon as a double-headed monster formerly was, or an honest publican. Ever since that epoch we have dropped the ridiculous employment of those inquiries about health with which the conversations of our ancestors were needlessly interlarded, such as "How are you?" or "How do you do?" Short-sightedness alone continued its lamentable progress, being stimulated by the extraordinary spread of journalism. There was not a woman or a child, who did not wear a *pince-nez*. This drawback, which besides was only momentary, was largely compensated for by the progress it caused in the optician's art.

Alongside of the political unity which did away with the enmities of nations, there appeared a linguistic unity which rapidly blotted out the last differences between them. Already since the twentieth century the need of a single common language, similar to Latin in the Middle Ages, had become sufficiently intense among the learned throughout the whole world to induce them to make use of an international idiom in all their writings. At the end of a long struggle for supremacy with English and Spanish, Greek finally established its claims, after the break-up of the British Empire and the recapture of Constantinople by the Græco-Russian Empire. Gradually, or rather with the rapidity characteristic of all modern progress, its usage descended from strata to strata till it reached the lowest layers of society, and from the middle of the twenty-second century there was not a little child between the Loire and the River Amour who could not express itself with ease in the language of Demosthenes. Here and there a few isolated villages in the hollows of the mountains still persisted, in spite of the protests of their schoolmasters, to mangle the old dialect formerly called French, German, or Italian, but the sound of this gibberish in the towns would have raised a hearty laugh.

All contemporary documents agree in bearing witness to the rapidity, the depth, and the universality of the change which took place in the customs, ideas, and needs, and in all the forms of social life, thus reduced to a common level from one pole to the other, as a result of this unification of language. It seemed as if the course of civilisation had been hitherto confined within high banks and that now, when for the first time all the banks had burst, it readily spread over the whole globe. It was no longer millions but thousands of millions that the least newly discovered improvement in industry brought in to its inventor; for henceforth there was no barrier to stop in its star-like radiation the expansion of any idea, no matter where it originated. For the same reason it was no longer by hundreds but by thousands, that were reckoned the editions of any book, which appealed but moderately to the public taste, or the performance of a play which was ever so little applauded. The rivalry between authors had therefore risen to its fullest diapason. Their fancy, moreover, could find full scope, for the first effect of this deluge of universalised neo-Hellenism had been to overwhelm for ever all the pretended literatures of our rude ancestors. They became unintelligible, even to the very titles of what they were pleased to call their classical masterpieces, even to the barbarous names of Shakespeare, Goethe, and Hugo, who are now forgotten, and whose rugged verses are deciphered with such difficulty by our scholars. To plagiarise these folks whom hardly anyone could henceforth read, was to render them service, nay, to pay them too much honour. One did not fail to do so; and prodigious was the success of these audacious imitations which were offered as original works. The material thus to turn to account was abundant, and indeed inexhaustible.

Unfortunately for the young writers the ancient poets who had been dead for centuries, Homer, Sophocles, Euripides, had returned to life, a hundred times more hale and hearty than at the time of

Pericles himself; and this unexpected competition proved a singular thorn in the side of the new-comers. It was in fact in vain that original geniuses produced on the stage such sensational novelties as *Athalias, Hernanias, Macbethès*; the public often turned its back on them to rush off to performances of *Oedipus Rex* or the *Birds* (of Aristophanes). And *Nanais*, though a vigorous sketch of a novelist of the new school, was a complete failure owing to the frenzied success of a popular edition of the Odyssey. The ears of the people were saturated with Alexandrines classical, romantic, and the rest. They were bored by the childish tricks of cæsura and rhyme which sometimes attempted a see-saw effect by producing now a poor and now a full rhyme, or again made a pretence of hiding away and keeping out of sight in order to induce the hearer to hunt it out. The splendid, untrammelled, and exuberant hexameters of Homer, the stanzas of Sappho, the iambics of Sophocles, furnished them with unspeakable pleasure, which did the greatest harm to the music of a certain Wagner. Music in general fell to the secondary position to which it really belongs in the hierarchy of the fine arts. To make up for it, in the midst of this scholarly renaissance of the human spirit, there arose an occasion for an unexpected literary outburst which allowed poetry to regain its legitimate rank, that is to say, the foremost. In fact it never fails to flower again when language takes a new lease of life, and all the more so when the latter undergoes a complete metamorphosis, and the pleasure arises of expressing anew the eternal truisms.

It was not merely a simple means of diversion for the cultured. The masses took their share in it with enthusiasm. Certainly they now had leisure to read and appreciate the masterpieces of art. The transmission of force at a distance by electricity, and its enlistment under a thousand forms, for instance, in that of cylinders of compressed air, which could be easily carried from place to place, had reduced manual labour to a mere nothing. The waterfalls, the winds and the tides had become the slaves of man, as steam had once been in the remote ages and in an infinitely less degree. Intelligently distributed and turned to account by means of improved machines, as simple as they were ingenious, this enormous energy freely furnished by nature had long rendered superfluous every kind of domestic servant and the greater number of artisans. The voluntary workmen, who still existed, spent barely three hours a day in the international factories, magnificent co-operative workshops, in which the productivity of human energy, multiplied tenfold, and even a hundredfold, surpassed the expectations of their founders.

This does not mean that the social problem had been thereby solved. In default of want, it is true, there were no longer any quarrels; wealth or a competence had become the lot of every man, with the result that hardly anyone henceforth set any store by them. In default of ugliness, also, love was scarcely an object of either appreciation or jealousy, owing to the abundance of pretty women and handsome men who were as common as blackberries and not difficult to please, in appearance at least. Thus expelled from its two former principal paths, human desire rushed with all its might towards the only field which remained open to it, the conquest of political power, which grew vaster every day owing to the progress of socialistic centralisation. Overflowing ambition, swollen all at once with all the evil passions pouring into it alone, with the covetousness, lust, envious hunger, and hungry envy of preceding ages, reached at that time an appalling height. It was a struggle as to who should make himself master of that *summum bonum*, the State; as to who should make the omnipotence and omniscience of the Universal State minister to the realisation of his personal programme or his humanitarian dreams. The result was not, as had been prophesied, a vast democratic republic. Such an immense outburst of pride could not fail to set up a new throne, the highest, the mightiest, the most glorious that has ever been. Besides, inasmuch as the population of the Single State was reckoned by thousands of millions, universal suffrage had become impracticable and illusory. To obviate the greater inconvenience of deliberative assemblies, ten or a hundred times too numerous, it had been found necessary so to increase the electoral districts that each deputy represented at least ten million electors. That is not surprising if one reflects that it was the first time that the very simple idea had won acceptance of extending to women and children the right of voting exercised in their name, naturally enough, by their father or by their lawful or natural husband. Incidentally one may note that this salutary and necessary reform, as much in accordance with common sense as with logic, required alike by the principle of national sovereignty and by the needs of social stability, nearly failed to pass, incredible as it may seem, in the face of a coalition of celibate electors.

Tradition informs us that the bill relating to this indispensable extension of the franchise would have been infallibly rejected, if, luckily, the recent election of a multi-millionaire suspected of imperialistic tendencies had not scared the assembly. It fancied it would injure the popularity of this ambitious pretender by hastening to welcome this proposal in which it only saw one thing, that is, that the fathers and husbands, outraged or alarmed by the gallantries of the new Cæsar, would be all the stronger for impeding his triumphant march. But this expectation was, it appears, unrealised.

Whatever may be the truth of this legend, it is certain that, owing to the enlargement of the electoral districts, combined with the suppression of the electoral privileges, the election of a deputy was a veritable coronation, and ordinarily produced in the elect a species of megalomania. This reconstituted feudalism was bound to end in a reconstitution of monarchy. For a moment the learned wore this cosmic crown, following the prophecy of an ancient philosopher, but they did not keep it. The popularisation of knowledge through innumerable schools had made science as common an object as a charming woman or an elegant suite of furniture. It had been extraordinarily simplified by the thorough way in which it had been worked out, complete as regards its general outlines, in which no change could be expected, and its henceforth rigid classification abundantly garnished with data. Only advancing at an imperceptible pace, it held, in short, but an insignificant place in the background of the brain, in which it simply replaced the catechism of former days. The bulk of intellectual energy was therefore to be found in another direction, as were also its glory and prestige. Already the scientific bodies, venerable in their antiquity, began, alas! to acquire a slight tinge and veneer of ridicule, which raised a smile and recalled the synods of bonzes or ecclesiastical conferences, such as are represented in very ancient pictures. It is, therefore, not surprising that this first dynasty of imperial physicists and geometricians, genial copies of the Antonines, were promptly succeeded by a dynasty of artists who had deserted art to wield the sceptre, as they lately had wielded the bow, the roughing chisel, and the brush. The most famous of all, a man possessed of an overflowing imagination which was yet well under control, and ministered to by an unparalleled energy, was an architect who among other gigantic projects formed the idea of rasing to the ground his capital, Constantinople, in order to rebuild it elsewhere, on the site of ancient Babylon, which for three thousand years had been a desert—a truly luminous idea. In this incomparable plain of Chaldea watered by a second Nile there was another still more beautiful and fertile Egypt awaiting resurrection and metamorphosis, an infinite expanse extending as far as the eye could see, to be covered with striking public buildings constructed with magical speed, with a teeming and throbbing population, with golden harvests beneath a sky of changeless blue, with an iron net-work of railways radiating from the town of Nebuchadnesor to the furthest ends of Europe, Africa and Asia, and crossing the Himalayas, the Caucasus, and the Sahara. The stored energy, electrically conveyed, of a hundred Abyssinian waterfalls, and of, I do not know, how many cyclones, hardly sufficed to transport from the mountains of Armenia the necessary stone, wood and iron for these numerous constructions. One day an excursion train, composed of a thousand and one carriages, having passed too close to the electric cable at the moment when the current was at its maximum, was destroyed and reduced to ashes in the twinkling of an eye. None the less Babylon, the proud city of muddy clay, with its paltry splendours of unbaked and painted brick, found itself rebuilt in marble and granite, to the utmost confusion of the Nabopolassars, the Belshazzars, the Cyruses, and the Alexanders. It is needless to add that the archæologists made on this occasion the most priceless discoveries, in the several successive strata, of Babylonian and Assyrian antiquities. The mania for Assyriology went so far that every sculptor's studio, the palaces, and even the King's armorial bearings were invaded by winged bulls with human heads, just as formerly the museums were full of cupids or cherubims, "with their cravat-like wings". Certain school books for primary schools were actually printed in cuneiform characters in order to enhance their authority over the youthful imagination.

This imperial orgy in bricks and mortar having unhappily occasioned the seventh, eighth, and ninth bankruptcy of the State and several consecutive inundations of paper-money, the people in general rejoiced to see after this brilliant reign the crown borne by a philosophical financier. Order had hardly been re-established in the finances, when he made his preparation for applying on a grand scale his ideal of government, which was of a highly remarkable nature. One was not long in noticing, in fact, after his accession, that all the newly chosen ladies of honour, who were otherwise very intelligent but entirely lacking in wit, were chiefly conspicuous for their striking ugliness; that the liveries of the court were of a grey and lifeless colour; that the court balls reproduced by instantaneous cinematography to the tune of millions of copies furnished a collection of the most honest and insignificant faces and unappetising forms that one could possibly see; that the candidates recently appointed, after a preliminary despatch of their portraits, to the highest dignities of the Empire, were pre-eminently distinguished by the commonness of their bearing; in short, that the races and the public holidays (the date of which were notified in advance by secret telegrams announcing the arrival of a cyclone from America), happened nine times out of ten to take place on a day of thick fog, or of pelting rain, which transformed them into an immense array of waterproofs and umbrellas. Alike in his legislative proposals, as in his appointments, the choice of the prince was always the following: the most useful and the best among the most unattractive. An insufferable sameness of colour, a depressing monotony, a sickening insipidity were the distinctive note of all the acts of the government. People laughed, grew excited, waxed indignant, and got used to it. The result was that at the end of a certain time it was impossible to meet an office-seeker or a politician, that is to say, an artist or literary man, out of his element and in search of the beautiful in an alien sphere, who did not turn his back on the pursuit of a government appointment in order to return to rhyming, sculpture and painting. And from that moment the following aphorism has won general acceptance, that the superiority of the politician is only mediocrity raised to its highest power.

This is the great benefit that we owe to this eminent monarch. The lofty purpose of his reign has been revealed by the posthumous publication of his memoirs. Of these writings with which we can so ill dispense, we have only left this fragment which is well calculated to make us regret the loss of the remainder: "Who is the true founder of Sociology? Auguste Comte? No, Menenius Agrippa. This great man understood that government is the stomach, not the head of the social organism. Now, the merit of a stomach is to be good and ugly, useful and repulsive to the eye, for if this indispensable organ were agreeable to look upon, it would be much to be feared that people would meddle with it and nature would not have taken such care to conceal and defend it. What sensible person prides himself on having a beautiful digestive apparatus, a lovely liver or elegant lungs? Such a pretension would, however, not be more ridiculous than the foible of cutting a great dash in politics. What wants cultivating is the substantial and the commonplace. My poor predecessors." ... Here follows a blank; a little further on, we read: "The best government is that which holds to being so perfectly humdrum, regular, neuter, and even emasculated, that no one can henceforth get up any enthusiasm either for or against it."

Such was the last successor of Semiramis. On the re-discovered site of the Hanging-gardens he caused to be erected, at the expense of the State, a statue of Louis Philippe in wrought aluminium, in the middle of a public garden planted with common laurels and cauliflowers.

The Universe breathed again. It yawned a little no doubt, but it revelled for the first time in the fulness of peace, in the almost gratuitous abundance of every kind of wealth. It burst into the most brilliant efflorescence, or rather display of poetry and art, but especially of luxury, that the world had as yet seen. It was just at that moment an extraordinary alarm of a novel kind, justly provoked by the astronomical observations made on the tower of Babel, which had been rebuilt as an Eiffel Tower on an enlarged scale, began to spread among the terrified populations.

II.
THE CATASTROPHE

On several occasions already the sun had given evident signs of weakness. From year to year his spots increased in size and number, and his heat sensibly diminished. People were lost in conjecture. Was his fuel giving out? Had he just traversed in his journey through space an exceptionally cold region? No one knew. Whatever the reason was, the public concerned itself little about the matter, as in all that is gradual and not sudden. The "solar anæmia," which moreover restored some degree of animation to neglected astronomy, had merely become the subject of several rather smart articles in the reviews. In general, the *savants*, in their well-warmed studies, affected to disbelieve in the fall of temperature, and, in spite of the formal indications of the thermometer, they did not cease to repeat that the dogma of slow evolution, and of the conservation of energy combined with the classical nebular hypothesis, forbade the admission of a sufficiently rapid cooling of the solar mass to make itself felt during the short duration of a century, much more so during that of five years or a year. A few unorthodox persons of heretical and pessimistic temperament remarked, it is true, that at different epochs, if one believed the astronomers of the remote past, certain stars had gradually burnt out in the heavens, or had passed from the most dazzling brilliance to an almost complete obscurity, during the course of barely a single year. They therefore concluded that the case of our sun had nothing exceptional about it; that the theory of slow-footed evolution was not perhaps universally applicable; and that, sometimes, as an old visionary mystic called Cuvier had ventured to put forward in legendary times, veritable revolutions took place in the heavens as well as on earth. But orthodox science combated with indignation these audacious theories.

However, the winter of 2489 was so disastrous, it was actually necessary to take the threatening predictions of the alarmists seriously. One reached the point of fearing at any moment a "solar apoplexy." That was the title of a sensational pamphlet which went through twenty thousand editions. The return of the spring was anxiously awaited.

The spring returned at last, and the starry monarch reappeared, but his golden crown was gone, and he himself well-nigh unrecognisable. He was entirely red. The meadows were no longer green, the sky was no longer blue, the Chinese were no longer yellow, all had suddenly changed colour as in a transformation scene. Then, by degrees, from the red that he was he became orange. He might then have been compared to a golden apple in the sky, and so during several years he was seen to pass, and all nature with him, through a thousand magnificent or terrible tints—from orange to yellow, from yellow to green, and from green at length to indigo and pale blue. The meteorologists then recalled the fact, in the year 1883, on the second of September, the sun had appeared in Venezuela the whole day long as blue as the moon. So many colours, so many new decorations of the chameleon-like universe which dazzled the terrified eye, which revived and restored to its primitive sharpness the rejuvenated sensation of the beauties of nature, and strongly stirred the depths of men's souls by renewing the former aspect of things.

At the same time disaster succeeded disaster. The entire population of Norway, Northern Russia, and Siberia perished, frozen to death in a single night; the temperate zone was decimated, and what was left of its inhabitants fled before the enormous drifts of snow and ice, and emigrated by hundreds of millions towards the tropics, crowding into the panting trains, several of which, overtaken by tornadoes of snow, disappeared for ever.

The telegraph successively informed the capital, now that there was no longer any news of immense trains caught in the tunnels under the Pyrenees, the Alps, the Caucasus, or Himalayas, in which they were imprisoned by enormous avalanches, which blocked simultaneously the two issues; now that some of the largest rivers of the world—the Rhine, for instance, and the Danube—had ceased to flow, completely frozen to the bottom, from which resulted a drought, followed by an indescribable famine, which obliged thousands of mothers to devour their own children. From time to time a country or continent broke off suddenly its communication with the central agency, the reason being that an entire telegraphic section was buried under the snow, from which at intervals emerged the uneven tops of their posts, with their little cups of porcelain. Of this immense network of electricity which enveloped in its close meshes the entire globe, as of that prodigious coat of mail with which the complicated system of railways clothed the earth, there was only left some scattered fragments, like the remnant of the Grand Army of Napoleon during the retreat from Russia.

Meanwhile, the glaciers of the Alps, the Andes, and of all the mountains of the world hitherto vanquished by the sun, which for several thousand centuries had been thrust back into their last entrenchments, resumed their triumphant march. All the glaciers that had been dead since the geological ages came to life again, more colossal than ever. From all the valleys in the Alps or Pyrenees, that were lately green and peopled with delightful health resorts, there issued these snowy hordes, these streams of icy lava, with their frontal moraine advancing as it spread over the plain, a moving cliff composed of rocks and overturned engines, of the wreckage of bridges, stations, hotels and public edifices, whirled along in the wildest confusion, a heart-breaking welter of gigantic bric-à-brac, with which the triumphant invasion decked itself out as with the loot of victory. Slowly, step by step, in spite of sundry transient intervals of light and warmth, in spite of occasionally scorching days which bore witness to the supreme convulsions of the sun in its battle against death, which revived in men's souls misleading hopes, athwart and even by means of these unexpected changes the pale invaders advanced. They retook and recovered one by one all their ancient realms in the glacial period, and if they found on the road some gigantic vagrant block lying in sullen solitude, near some famous city, a hundred leagues from its native hills, mysterious witness of the immense catastrophe of former times, they raised it and bore it onward, cradling it on their unyielding waves, as an advancing army recaptures and enfurls its ancient flags, all covered with dust, which it has found again in its enemies' sanctuaries.

But what was the glacial period compared with this new crisis of the globe and the sky? Doubtless it had been due to a similar attack of weakness, to a similar failure of the sun, and many species of animals had necessarily perished at the time, from being insufficiently clad. That had been, however, but a warning bell, so to say, a simple notification of the final and fatal attack. The glacial periods—for we know there have been several—now explained themselves by their reappearance on a large scale. But this clearing up of an obscure point in geology was, one must admit, an insufficient compensation for the public disasters which were its price.

What calamities! What horrors! My pen confesses its impotence to retrace them. Besides how can we tell the story of disasters which were so complete they often simultaneously overwhelmed under snow-drifts a hundred yards deep all that witnessed them, to the very last man. All that we know for certain is what took place at the time towards the end of the twenty-fifth century in a little district of Arabia Petræa.

Thither had flocked for refuge, in one horde after another, wave after wave, with host upon host frozen one on the top of another, as they advanced, the few millions of human creatures who survived of the hundreds of millions that had disappeared. Arabia Petræa had, therefore, along with the Sahara, become the most populous country of the globe. They transported hither by reason of the relative warmth of its climate, I will not say the seat of Government—for, alas! Terror alone reigned—but an immense stove which took its place, and whatever remained of Babylon now covered over by a glacier. A new town was constructed in a few months on the plans of an entirely new system of architecture, marvellously adapted for the struggle against the cold. By the most happy of chances some rich and unworked coal mines were discovered on the spot. There was enough fuel there, it seems, to provide warmth for many years to come. And as for food, it was not as yet too pressing a question. The granaries contained several sacks of corn, while waiting for the sun to revive and the corn to sprout again. The sun had certainly revived after the glacial periods; why should it not do so again? asked the optimists.

It was but the hope of a day. The sun assumed a violet hue. The frozen corn ceased to be eatable. The cold became so intense that the walls of the houses as they contracted cracked and admitted blasts of air which killed the inhabitants on the spot. A physicist affirmed that he saw crystals of solid nitrogen and oxygen fall from the sky which gave rise to the fear that the atmosphere would shortly become decomposed. The seas were already frozen solid. A hundred thousand human creatures huddling around the huge government stove, which was no longer equal to restoring their circulation, were turned into icicles in a single night; and the night following, a second hundred thousand perished likewise. Of the beautiful human race, so strong and noble, formed by so many centuries of effort and genius by such an intelligent and extended selection, there would soon have been only left a few thousands, a few hundreds of haggard and trembling specimens, unique trustees of the last ruins of what had once been civilisation.

III.
THE STRUGGLE

In this extremity a man arose who did not despair of humanity. His name has been preserved for us. By a singular coincidence he was called Miltiades, like another saviour of Hellenism. He was not, however, of Hellenic race. A cross between a Slave and a Breton he had only half sympathised with the prosperity of the Neo-Græcian world with its levelling and enervating tendencies, and amid this wholesale obliteration of previous civilisation, and universal triumph of a kind of Byzantine renaissance brought up to date, he belonged to those who reverently guarded in the depths of their heart the germs of recusancy. But, like the barbarian stilicho, the last defender of the foundering Roman world against the barbaric hordes, it was precisely this disbeliever in civilisation who alone undertook to arrest it on the brink of its vast downfall. Eloquent and handsome, but nearly always taciturn, he was not without certain resemblances in pose and features, so it was said, to Chateaubriand and Napoleon (two celebrities, as one knows, who in their time were famous throughout an entire continent). Worshipped by the women of whom he was the hope, and by the men who stood greatly in awe of him, he had early kept the crowd at arm's length, and a singular accident had doubled his natural shyness. Finding the sea less monotonously dull at any rate than terra firma, and in any case more unconfined, he had passed his youth on board the last iron-clad of State of which he was captain, in patrolling the coasts of continents, in dreaming of impossible adventures, and of conquests when all was conquered, of discoveries of America when all was discovered, and in cursing all former travellers, discoverers and conquerors, fortunate reapers in all the fields of glory in which there was nothing more left to glean. One day, however, he believed he had discovered a new island—it was a mistake—and he had the joy of engaging in a fight, the last of which ancient history makes mention, with an apparently highly primitive tribe of savages, who spoke English and read the Bible. In this fight he displayed such valour that he was unanimously pronounced to be mad by his crew, and was in great danger of losing his rank after a specialist in insanity, who had been called in, was on the point of publicly confirming popular opinion by declaring he was suffering from suicidal mono-mania of a novel kind. Luckily an archæologist protested and showed by actual documents that this phenomenon, which had become so unusual but was frequent in past ages under the name of bravery, was a simple case of ancestral reversion sufficiently serious to merit examination. As luck would have it, the unfortunate Miltiades had been wounded in the face in the same encounter; and the scar which all the art of the best surgeons never succeeded in removing, drew down upon him the annoying and almost insulting nick-name of "scarred face". It may be readily understood how from this time forward, soured by the consciousness of his partial disfigurement, as the ancient bard Byron had formerly been for a nearly similar reason, he avoided appearing in public, and thereby giving the crowd an opportunity of pointing the finger of scorn at the visible traces of his former attack of madness. He was never seen again till the day when, his vessel being hemmed in by the icebergs of the Gulf Stream, he was obliged with his companions to finish the crossing on foot over the solidly frozen Atlantic.

In the middle of the central state shelter, a huge vaulted hall with walls ten yards thick, without windows, surrounded with a hundred gigantic furnaces, and perpetually lit up by their hundred flaming maws, Miltiades one day appeared. The remnant of the flower of humanity, of both sexes, splendid even in its misery, was huddled together there. They did not consist of the great men of science with their bald pates, nor even the great actresses, nor the great writers, whose inspiration had deserted them, nor the consequential ones now past their prime, nor of prim old ladies—broncho-pneumonia, alas! had made a clean sweep of them all at the very first frost—but the enthusiastic heirs of their traditions, their secrets, and also of their vacant chairs, that is to say, their pupils, full of talent and promise. Not a single university professor was there, but a crowd of deputies and assistants; not a single minister, but a crowd of young secretaries of state. Not a single mother of a family, but a bevy of artists' models, admirably formed, and inured against the cold by the practice of posing for the nude; above all, a number of fashionable beauties, who had been likewise saved by the excellent hygienic effect of daily wearing low dresses, without taking into account the warmth of their temperament. Among them it was impossible not to notice the Princess Lydia, owing to her tall and exquisite figure, the brilliancy of her dress and her wit, of her dark eyes and fair complexion, owing in fact to the radiance of her whole person. She had carried off the prize at the last grand international beauty competition, and was accounted the reigning beauty of the drawing-rooms of Babylon. What a different set of individuals from that which the spectator formerly surveyed through his opera-glass from the top of the galleries of the so-called Chamber of Deputies! Youth, beauty, genius, love, infinite treasures of science and art, writers whose pens were of pure gold, artists with marvellous technique, singers one raved about, all that was left of refinement and culture on the earth, was concentrated in this last knot of human beings, which blossomed under the snow like a tuft of rhododendrons, or of Alpine roses at the foot of some mountain summit. But what dejection had fallen on these fair flowers! How sadly drooped these manifold graces!

At the sudden apparition of Miltiades every brow was lifted, every eye was fastened upon him. He was tall, lean, and wizened, in spite of the false plumpness of his thick white furs. When he threw back his big white hood, which recalled the Dominican cowl of antiquity, they caught sight of his huge scar athwart the icicles on his beard and eyebrows. At the sight of it first a smile and then a shudder, which was not due to cold alone, ran through the ranks of the women. For must we confess it, in spite of the efforts of a rational education, the inclination to applaud bravery and its indications could not be entirely uprooted from their hearts. Lydia, notably, remained imbued with this sentiment of another age, by a kind of moral ancestral reversion which served as a pendant to her physical atavism. She concealed so little her feelings of admiration, that Miltiades himself was struck by it. Her admiration was combined with astonishment, for he was believed to have been dead for years. They asked one another by what accumulation of miracles he had been able to escape the fate of his companions. He requested leave to speak. It was granted him. He mounted a platform, and such a profound silence ensued, one might have heard the snow falling outside, in spite of the thickness of the walls. But let us at this point allow an eye-witness to speak; let us copy an extract of the account that he phonographed of this memorable scene. I pass over the part of Miltiades' discourse in which he related the thrilling story of the dangers he had encountered from the time he left his vessel. (*Continuous applause.*) After stating that in passing by Paris on a sledge drawn by reindeer—thanks to it being the season of the dog-days—he had recognised the site of this buried city by the double-pointed mound of snow which had formed over the spires of Notre-Dame—(*excitement in the audience*)—the speaker continued:—

"The situation is serious," said he, "nothing like it has been seen since the geological epochs. Is it irretrievable? No! (*Hear! hear!*) Desperate diseases require desperate remedies. An idea, a glimmer of hope has flashed upon me, but it is so strange, I shall never dare to reveal it to you. (*Speak! speak!*) No, I dare not, I shall never dare to formulate this project. You would believe me to be still insane. You desire it, you promise me to listen to the end to my absurd and extravagant project? (*Yes! yes!*) Even to give it a fair trial? (*Yes! yes!*) Well! I will speak. (*Silence!*)

"The hour has come to ascertain to what extent it is true to say and to keep on repeating, as has been the practice for the last three centuries since the time of a certain Stephenson, that all our energy, all our strength, whether physical or moral, comes to us from the sun.... (*Numerous voices: 'That is so'*). The calculation has been made: in two years, three months, and six days, if there still remains a morsel of coal there will not remain a morsel of bread! (*Prolonged sensation.*) Therefore, if the source of all force, of all motion, and all life is in the sun, and in the sun alone, there is no ground for self-delusion: in two years, three months, and six days, the genius of man will be quenched, and through the gloomy heavens the corpse of mankind, like a Siberian mammoth, will roll for everlasting, incapable for ever of resurrection. (*Excitement.*)

"But is that the case? No, it is not, it cannot be the case. With all the energy of my heart, which does not come from the sun—that energy which comes from the earth, from our mother earth buried there below, far, far away, for ever hidden from our eyes—I protest against this vain theory, and against so many articles of faith and religion which I have been obliged hitherto to endure in silence. (*Slight murmurs from the centre.*) The earth is the contemporary of the sun, and not its daughter; the earth was formerly a luminous star like the sun, only sooner extinct. It is only on the surface that the earth is devoid of movement, frozen and paralysed. Its bosom is ever warm and burning. It has only concentrated its fire within itself in order to preserve it better. (*Signs of interest in the audience.*) There lies a virgin force that is unexploited, a force superior to all that the sun has been able to generate for our industry by waterfalls which to-day are frozen, by cyclones which now have ceased, by tides which to-day are suspended; a force in which our engineers, with a little initiative, will find a hundredfold the equivalent of the motive power they have lost. It is no more by this gesture (*the speaker raises his finger to heaven*), that the hope of salvation should henceforth be expressed, it is by this one. (*He lowers his right hand towards the earth.... Signs of astonishment: a few murmurs of dissent which are immediately repressed by the women.*) We must say no more: 'Up there!' but, 'below!' There, below, far below, lies the promised Eden, the abode of deliverance and of bliss: there, and there alone, there are still innumerable conquests and discoveries to be made! (*Bravos on the left.*) Ought I to draw my conclusion? (*Yes! yes!*) Let us descend into these depths; let us make these abysses our sure retreat. The mystics had a sublime presentiment when they said in their Latin: 'From the outward to the inward.' The earth calls us to its inner self. For many centuries it has lived separated, so to say, from its children, the living creatures it produced outside during its period of fecundity before the cooling of its crust! After its crust cooled, the rays of a distant star alone, it is true, have maintained on this dead epidermis their artificial and superficial life which has been a stranger to her own.

"But this schism has lasted too long. It is imperative that it should cease. It is time to follow Empedocles, Ulysses, Æneas, Dante, to the gloomy abodes of the underworld, to plunge mankind again in the fountain from which it sprang, to effect the complete restoration of the exiled soul to the land of its birth! (*Applause here and there.*) Besides, there is but this alternative: life underground or death. The sun is failing us: let us dispense with the sun. The plan, which it remains for me to propose, has been worked out for several months past by the most eminent men. To-day it is finished; it is final. It is complete in all its details. Does it interest you? (*On all sides: 'Read it, read it.'*) You will see that with discipline, patience, and courage—yes, courage, I risk this evil-sounding word (*'Risk it, risk it.'*)—and above all, with the aid of that splendid heritage of science and art which comes to us from the past, for which we are accountable to the most distant of our descendants, to the boundless universe, and I was going to say, to God (*signs of surprise*), we can be saved if we will." (*Thunder of applause.*)

The speaker next entered into lengthy details, which it is useless to reproduce here, on the Neo-troglodytism which he pretended to inaugurate as the acme of civilisation, "which had," said he, "began with caves, and was destined to return to these subterranean retreats, but at a far deeper level." He displayed designs, quantities and drawings. He had no trouble in proving that, on condition of burrowing sufficiently deep into the ground below, they would find a deliciously gentle warmth, an Elysian temperature. It would be enough to excavate, enlarge, heighten, and extend the galleries of already existing mines in order to render them habitable and comfortable into the bargain. The electric light, supplied entirely without expense by the scattered centres of the fire within, would provide for the magnificent illumination both by day and night of these colossal crypts, these marvellous cloisters, indefinitely extended and embellished by successive generations. With a good system of ventilation, all danger of suffocation or of foulness of air would be avoided. In short, after a more or less long period of settling in, civilised life could unfold anew in all its intellectual, artistic, and fashionable splendour, as freely as it did in the capricious and intermittent light or natural day, and even perhaps more surely. At these last words, the Princess Lydia broke her fan, by dint of applauding. An objection then came from the right, "With what shall we be fed?" Miltiades smiled disdainfully and replied: "Nothing is simpler. For ordinary drinking purposes we first of all shall have melted ice. Every day we shall transport enormous blocks of it in order to keep the orifices of the crypts free from obstruction, and to supply the public fountains. I may add that chemists undertake to manufacture alcohol from anything, even from mineralised rocks, and that it is the A.B.C. of the grocer's trade to manufacture wine from alcohol and water. (*'Hear! hear!' from all the benches*). As for food, is not chemistry also capable of manufacturing butter, albumen, and milk from no matter what? Besides, has the last word been said on the subject? Is it not highly probable that before long, if it takes up the matter, it will succeed in satisfying, both on the score of quantity and expense, the desires of the most refined gastronomy? And, meanwhile.... (*a voice timidly:* '*Meanwhile?*') Meanwhile does not our disaster itself, by a kind of providential occurrence, place within our reach the best stocked, the most abundant, the most inexhaustible larder that the human race has ever had? Immense stores, the most admirable which have hitherto been laid down, are lying for us under the ice or the snow. Myriads of domestic or wild animals—I dare not add, of men and women (*a general shudder of horror*)—but at least of bullocks, sheep and poultry, frozen instantaneously in a single mass, are lying here and there in the public markets a few steps away. Let us collect, as long as such work is still possible out of doors, this boundless quarry which was destined to feed for years several hundreds of millions, and which will well suffice, in consequence, to feed a few thousands only for ages, even should they multiply unduly, in despite of Malthus. If stacked in the neighbourhood of the orifice of the chief cavern, they will be easy to get at and will provide a delightful fare for our fraternal love-feasts."

Still further objections were formulated from different quarters. They were forcibly disposed of with the same irresistible easy assurance. The conclusion is worthy of a verbatim quotation: "However extraordinary the catastrophe which has befallen us and the means of escape which is left us may seem in appearance, a little reflection will suffice to prove to us that the predicament in which we are, must have been repeated a thousand times already in the immensity of the universe, and must have been cleared up in the same fashion, being inevitably and normally the final phase in the life-drama of every star. The astronomers know that every sun is bound to become extinct; they know, therefore, that in addition to the luminous and visible stars, there are in the heavens an infinitely greater number of extinct and rayless stars which continue endlessly to revolve with their train of planets, doomed to an eternity of night and cold. Well, if this is the case, I ask you: Can we suppose that life, thought, and love, are the exclusive privilege of an infinite minority of solar systems still possessed of light and heat, and deny to the immense majority of gloomy stars every manifestation of life and animation, the very highest reason for their existence? Thus lifelessness, death, the void in movement would be the rule; and life the exception! Thus the nine-tenths, the ninety-nine hundredths, perhaps, of the solar systems, would idly revolve like senseless and gigantic mill-wheels, a useless encumbrance of space. That is impossible and idiotic, that is blasphemous. Let us have more faith in the unknown! Truth, here as everywhere else, is without doubt the antipodes of appearance. All that glitters is not gold. These splendid constellations which attempt to dazzle us are themselves relatively barren. Their light, what is it? A transient glory, a ruinous luxury, an ostentatious squandering of energy, born of illimitable senselessness. But when the stars have sown their wild oats, then the serious task of their life begins, they develop their inner resources. For frozen and sunless without, they literally preserve in their inviolate centres their unquenchable fire, defended by the very layers of ice. There, finally, is to be relit the lamp of life, banished from the surface above. For a last time, therefore, let us look upwards in order there to find hope. Up there innumerable races of mankind under ground, buried, to their supreme joy, in the catacombs of invisible stars, encourage us by their example. Let us act like them, let us like them withdraw to the interior of our planet. Like them, let us bury ourselves in order to rise again, and like them let us carry with us into our tomb, all that is worthy to survive of our previous existence. It is not merely bread alone that man has need of. He must live to think, and not merely think to live.

"Recall the legend of Noah: to escape from a disaster almost equal to our own, and to dispute with it all that the earth had most precious in his eyes; what did he do, though he was but a simple-minded fellow and addicted to drink? He turned his ark into a museum, containing a complete collection of plants and animals, even of poisonous plants, of wild beasts, boa-constrictors, and scorpions, and by reason of this picturesque but incongruous cargo of creatures mutually harmful and seeking one and all to devour each other, of this miscellany of living contradictions which for so long was so foolishly worshipped under the name of Nature, he believed in good faith to have deserved well of the future.

"But we, in our new ark, mysterious, impenetrable, indestructible, shall carry with us neither plants nor animals. These types of existence are annihilated; these rough drafts in creation, these fumbling experiments of Earth in quest of the human form are for ever blotted out. Let us not regret it. In place of so many pairs of animals which take up so much room, of so many useless seeds, we will carry with us into our retreat the harmonious garland of all the truths in perfect accord with one another; of all artistic and poetic beauties, which are all members one of another, united like sisters, which human genius has brought to light in the course of ages and multiplied thereafter in millions of copies: all of which will be destroyed save a single one, which it will be our task to guarantee against all danger of destruction. We shall establish a vast library containing all the principal works, enriched with cinematographic albums. We shall set up a vast museum composed of single specimens of all the schools, of all the styles of the masters in architecture, sculpture, painting, and even music. These are our real treasures, our real seed for future harvests, our gods for whom we will do battle till our latest breath."

The speaker stepped down from the platform in the midst of indescribable enthusiasm: the ladies crowded round him. They deputed Lydia to bestow on him a kiss in the name of them all. Blushing with modesty the latter obeyed—a further sign of moral atavism on her part—and the applause redoubled. The thermometers of the shelter rose several degrees in a few minutes.

It is well to recall to the younger generation these resolute words, between the lines of which they will read the gratitude they owe to the heroic "Scarred face," who so nearly died with the reputation of a mono-maniac. They, too, are beginning to grow enervated and accustomed to the delights of their underground Elysium, to the luxurious spaciousness of these endless catacombs, the legacy of gigantic toil on the part of their fathers, they too, are, inclined to think that all this happened of its own accord, or at least was inevitable, that after all there was no other way of escaping from the cold above ground, and that this simple expedient did not require a great outlay of imagination. Profound error! At its first appearance, the idea of Miltiades had been hailed, and rightly enough, as a flash of genius. But for him, but for his energy, and his eloquence, which was placed at the service of his imagination, but for his forcefulness, his charm, and his perseverance, which seconded his energy, let us add, but for the profound passion that Lydia, the noblest and most valiant of women, had been able to inspire in him, and which increased his heroism tenfold, humanity would have suffered the fate of all the other animal or vegetable species. What strikes us to-day in his discourse is the extraordinary and truly prophetic lucidity with which he sketched in general terms the conditions of existence in the new world. Without doubt, these expectations have been immensely surpassed. He did not foresee, he could not foresee, the prodigious accessions which his original idea has received owing to its development by thousands of auxiliary geniuses. He was far more right than he fancied, like the majority of reformers—who are generally wrongly accused, of being too much wrapt up in their own ideas. But on the whole, never was so magnificent a plan so promptly carried out.

From that very day all these exquisite and delicate hands set to work, aided, it is true, by incomparable machines. Everywhere, at the head of all the workings, were to be found Lydia and Miltiades. Henceforth inseparable, they vied with one another in ardour; and before a year was out the galleries of the mines had become sufficiently large and comfortable, sufficiently decorated even and brilliantly lighted, to receive the vast and priceless collections of all kinds, which it was their object to place in safety there, in view of the future.

With infinite precautions they were lowered one after another, bale by bale, into the bowels of the earth. This salvage of the goods and chattels of humanity was methodically carried out. It included all the quintessence of the ancient grand libraries of Paris, Berlin, and London, which had been brought together at Babylon, and then carried for safety into the desert with the rest. The cream of all former museums, of all previous exhibitions of industry and art, was concentrated there with considerable additions. There were manuscripts, books, bronzes, and pictures. What an expenditure of energy and incessant toil, in spite of the assistance of inter-terrestrial forces, had been necessary for packing, transporting, and housing it all! And yet, for the greater part, it was useless to those who voluntarily this task imposed upon themselves. They all knew it. They were well aware that they were probably condemned for the rest of their days to a hard and matter-of-fact existence, for which their lives as artists, philosophers, and men of letters, had scarcely prepared them. But—for the first time—the idea of duty to be done found its way into these hearts, the beauty of self-sacrifice subdued these dilettanti. They sacrificed themselves to the Unknown, to that which is not yet, to the posterity towards which were turned all the desires of their electrified spirits, as all the atoms of the magnetised iron turn towards the pole. It was thus that, at the time when there were still countries, in the midst of some great national peril, a wave of heroism swept over the most frivolous cities. However admirable may have been, at the epoch of which I speak, this collective need of individual self-sacrifice, ought we to be astonished at it, when we know from the treatises on natural history that have been preserved, that mere insects giving the same example of foresight and self-renunciation, used before their death to employ their latest energies to collect provisions useless to themselves, and only useful in the future to their larvæ at their birth.

IV.

SAVED!

The day at length arrived on which, all the intellectual inheritance of the past, all the real capital of humanity having been rescued from the general shipwreck, the castaways were able to go down in their turn, having henceforth only to think of their own preservation. That day which forms, as everyone knows, the starting point of our new era, called the era of salvation, was a solemn holiday. The sun, however, as if to arouse regret, indulged in a few last bursts of sunshine. On casting a final glance on this brightness, which they were never to behold again, the survivors of mankind could not, we are told, restrain their tears. A young poet on the brink of the pit that yawned to swallow them up, repeated in the musical language of Euripides, the farewell to the light of the dying Iphigenia. But that was a short-lived moment of very natural emotion which speedily changed into an outburst of unspeakable delight.

How great in fact was their amazement and their ecstasy! They expected a tomb; they opened their eyes in the most brilliant and interminable galleries of art they could possibly see, in *salons* more beautiful than those of Versailles, in enchanted palaces, in which all extremes of climate, rain, and wind, cold and torrid heat were unknown; where innumerable lamps, veritable suns in brilliancy and moons in softness, shed unceasingly through the blue depths their daylight that knew no night. Assuredly the sight was far from what it has since become; we need an effort of imagination in order to represent the psychological condition of our poor ancestors, hitherto accustomed to the perpetual and insufferable discomforts and inconveniences of life on the surface of the globe, in order to realise their enthusiasm, at a moment, when only counting on escaping from the most appalling of deaths by means of the gloomiest of dungeons, they felt themselves delivered of all their troubles, and of all their apprehensions at the same time! Have you noticed in the retrospective museum that quaint bit of apparatus of our fathers, which is called an umbrella? Look at it and reflect on the heart-breaking element, in a situation, which condemned man to make use of this ridiculous piece of furniture. Imagine yourself obliged to protect yourselves against those gigantic downpours which would unexpectedly arrive on the scene and drench you for three or four days running. Think likewise of sailors caught in a whirling cyclone, of the victims of sunstroke, of the 20,000 Indians annually devoured by tigers or killed by the bite of venomous serpents; think of those struck by lightning. I do not speak of the legions of parasites and insects, of the acarus, the phylloxera, and the microscopic beings which drained the blood, the sweat, and the life of man, inoculating him with typhus, plague, and cholera. In truth, if our change of condition has demanded some sacrifices, it is not an illusion to declare that the balance of advantage is immensely greater. What in comparison with this unparalleled revolution is the most renowned of the petty revolutions of the past which to-day are treated so lightly, and rightly so, by our historians. One wonders how the first inhabitants of these underground dwellings could, even for a moment, regret the sun, a mode of lighting that bristled with so many inconveniences. The sun was a capricious luminary which went out and was relit at variable hours, shone when it felt disposed, sometimes was eclipsed, or hid itself behind the clouds when one had most need of it, or pitilessly blinded one at the very moment one yearned for shade! Every night,—do we really realise the full force of the inconvenience?—every night the sun commanded social life to desist and social life desisted. Humanity was actually to that extent the slave of nature! To think it never succeeded in, never even dreamed of, freeing itself from this slavery which weighed so heavily and unconsciously on its destinies, on the course of its progress thus straitened and confined! Ah! Let us once more bless our fortunate disaster!

    What excuses or explains the weakness of the first immigrants of the inner world is the fact that their life was necessarily rough and full of hardships, in spite of a notable improvement after their descent into the caverns. They had perpetually to enlarge them, to adjust them to the requirements of the two civilisations, ancient and modern. That was not the work of a single day. I am well aware how happily fortune favoured them; how they again and again had the good luck when driving their tunnels to discover natural grottoes of the utmost beauty, in which it was enough to illuminate with the usual methods of lighting (which was absolutely cost-free, as Miltiades had foreseen) in order to render them almost habitable: delightful squares, as it were, enshrined and sparsely disseminated throughout the labyrinth of our brilliantly lighted streets; mines of sparkling diamonds, lakes of quicksilver, mounds of golden ingots. I am well aware that they had at their disposition a sum of natural forces very superior to all that the preceding ages had been acquainted with. That is very easy to understand. In fact, if they lacked waterfalls, they replaced them very advantageously by the finest falls in temperature that physicists have ever dreamed of. The central heat of the globe could not, it is true, by itself alone be a mechanical force, any more than formerly a large mass of water falling by hypothesis to the greatest possible depth. It is in its passage from a higher to a lower level that the mass of water becomes (or rather became) available energy: it is in its descent from a higher to a lower degree of the thermometer that heat likewise becomes so. The greater distance between any two degrees the greater amount of surplus energy. Now, the mining physicists had hardly descended into the bowels of the earth ere they at once perceived that thus placed between the furnaces of the central fire, as it were, a forge of the Cyclops, hot enough to liquefy granite, and the outer cold, which was sufficient to solidify oxygen and nitrogen, they had at their disposal the most enormous extremes in temperature, and consequently thermic cataracts by the side of which all the cataracts of Abyssinia and Niagara were only toys. What caldrons did they own in the ancient volcanoes! What condensers in the glaciers! At first sight they must have seen that if a few distributing agencies of this prodigious energy were provided, they had power enough there to perform the whole work of mankind—excavation, air supply, water supply, sanitation, locomotion, descent and transport of provisions, etc.

I am well aware of that. I am further aware that ever favoured by fortune, the inseparable friend of daring, the new Troglodytes have never suffered from famine, nor from shortness of supplies. When one of their snow-covered deposits of carcasses threatened to give out, they used to make several trial borings, drive several shafts in an upward direction. They never failed presently to meet with rich finds of food reserves, extensive enough to close the mouths of the alarmists, whereby there resulted on each occasion, according to the law of Malthus, a sudden increase in the population, coupled with the excavation of new underground cities, more flourishing than their older sisters. But, in spite of all this, we remain overwhelmed with wonder when we consider the incalculable degree of courage and intelligence lavished on such a work, and solely called into being by an idea which, starting one day from one individual brain, has leavened the whole globe. What giant falls of earth, what murderous explosions, what a death-roll there must have been at the outset of the enterprise! We shall never know what bloodthirsty duels, what rapes, what doleful tragedies, took place in this lawless society, which had not yet been reorganised. The history of the early conquerors and colonists of America, if it could be told in detail, would pale entirely beside it. Let us draw a veil over the proceedings. But this pitch of horrors was perhaps necessary to teach us that in the forced intimacy of a cave there is no mean between warfare and love, between mutual slaughter or mutual embraces. We began by fighting; to-day we fall on each other's necks. And in fact, what human ear, nose, or stomach could have longer withstood the deafening roar and smoke of melanite explosions beneath our crypts; the sight and stench of mangled bodies piled up within our narrow confines? Hideous and odious, revolting beyond all expression, the underground war finished by becoming impossible.

It is, however, painful to think that it lasted right up to the death of our glorious preserver. Everyone is acquainted with the heroic adventure in which Miltiades and his companion lost their lives. It has been so often painted, sculptured, sung, and immortalised by the great masters, that it is not allowable to pass it over in silence. The famous struggle between the centralist and federalist cities, that is to say, at bottom, between the industrial and artist cities, having ended in the triumph of the latter, a still more bloodthirsty conflict sprang up between the free thinking and the cellular cities. The former fought to assert the freedom of love with its uncertain fecundity; the second, for its prudent regulation. Miltiades, misled by his passion, committed the fault of siding with the former, a pardonable error which posterity has forgiven him. Besieged in his last grotto—a perfect marvel in strongholds—and at the end of his provisions, the besiegers having intercepted the arrival of all his convoys, he essayed a final effort: he prepared a formidable explosion intended to blow up the vault of his cavern, and forcibly to open a way upwards by which he might have the chance of reaching a deposit of provisions. His hope was deceived. The vault blew up, it is true, and disclosed a cavern above it, the most colossal one had hitherto seen, that dimly resembled a Hindoo temple. But the hero himself perished miserably, buried with Lydia beneath enormous rocks on the very spot on which now stands their double statue in marble, the masterpiece of our new Phidias, which is now the crowded meeting-place of our national pilgrimages.

From these fruitful though troublous times, and from this beneficial disorder, an advantage has accrued to us which we shall never sufficiently appreciate. Our race, already so beautiful, has been further strengthened and purified by these numerous trials. Short-sightedness itself has disappeared under the prolonged influence of a light that is pleasing to the eye, and of the habit of reading books which are written in very large characters. For, from lack of paper, we are obliged to write on slates, on pillars, obelisks, on the broad panels of marble, and this necessity, in addition to compelling us to adopt a sober style and contributing to the formation of taste, prevents the daily newspapers from reappearing, to the great benefit of the optic nerves and the lobes of the brain. It was, by the way, an immense misfortune for "pre-salvationist" man to possess textile plants which allowed him to stereotype without the slightest trouble on rags of paper without the slightest value, all his ideas, idle or serious, piled indiscriminately one on the other. Now, before graving our thoughts on a panel of rock, we take time to reflect on our subject. Yet another bane among our primitive forefathers was tobacco. At present we no longer smoke, we can no longer smoke. The public health is accordingly magnificent.

V.
REGENERATION

It does not fall within the scope of my rapid sketch to relate date by date the laborious vicissitudes of humanity since its settlement within the planet from the year 1 of the era of Salvation to the year 596, in which I write these lines in chalk on slabs of schist. I should only like to bring out for my contemporaries, who might very well fail to notice them (for we barely observe what we have always before our eyes), the distinctive and original features of this modern civilisation of which we are so justly proud. Now that after many abortive trials and agonizing convulsions it has succeeded in taking its final shape, we can clearly establish its essential characteristics. It consists in the complete elimination of living nature, whether animal or vegetable, man only excepted. That has produced, so to say, a purification of society. Secluded thus from every influence of the natural milieu into which it was hitherto plunged and confined, the social milieu was for the first time able to reveal and display its true virtues, and the real social bond appeared in all its vigour and purity. It might be said that destiny had desired to make in our case an extended sociological experiment for its own edification by placing us in such extraordinarily unique conditions. [1] The problem, in a way, was to learn, what would social man become if committed to his own keeping, yet left to himself—furnished with all the intellectual acquisitions accumulated through a remote past by human geniuses, but deprived of the assistance of all other living beings, nay, even of those beings half endowed with life, that we call rivers and seas and stars, and thrown back on the conquered, yet passive forces of chemical, inorganic and lifeless Nature, which is separated from man by too deep a chasm to exercise on him any action from the social point of view. The problem was to learn what this humanity would do when restricted to man, and obliged to extract from its own resources, if not its food supplies, yet at least all its pleasures, all its occupations, all its creative inspirations. The answer has been given, and we have realised at the same time what an unsuspected drag the terrestrial fauna and flora had hitherto been on the progress of humanity.

[1] In appearance only: we must not forget that in accordance with all probability many extinct stars must have served as the scene of this normal and necessary phase of social life.

At first human pride and the faith of man in himself hitherto held in check by the constant presence, by the profound sense of the superiority of the forces round it, rebounded with a force of elasticity really appalling. We are a race of Titans. But, at the same time, whatever enervating element there might have been in the air of our grottoes has been thereby victoriously combated. Otherwise our air is the purest that man has ever breathed; all the bad germs with which the atmosphere was loaded were killed by the cold. Far from being attacked by anæmia as some predicted, we live in a state of habitual excitement maintained by the multiplicity of our relations and of our "social tonics" (friendly shakes of the hand, talks, meetings with charming women, etc.). With a certain number among us it passes into a state of unintermittent delirium under the name of Troglodytic fever. This new malady, whose microbe has not yet been discovered, was unknown to our forefathers, thanks perhaps to the stupefying (or soothing, if you prefer it) influence of natural and rural distractions. Rural! what a strange anachronism! Fishermen, hunters, ploughmen, and shepherds—do we really understand to-day the meaning of these words? Have we for a moment reflected on the life of that fossil creature who is so frequently mentioned in books of ancient history and who was called the peasant? The habitual society of this curious creature which comprised half or three-quarters of the population was not man, but four-footed beasts, pot herbs and green crops, which, owing to the conditions necessary for their production in the country (yet another word which has become meaningless) condemned him to live a wild, solitary life, far from his fellows. As for his herds, they were acquainted with the charms of social life, but he had not the slightest inkling of what it meant.

The towns, to which people were so astonished that there should be a desire to emigrate, were the only centres, rare and widely scattered as they were, in which life in society was then known. But to what extent does it not appear to have been adulterated, and attenuated by animal and vegetable life? Another fossil peculiar to these regions is the artisan. Was the relation of the worker to his employer, of the artisan class to the other classes of the population, of these classes between themselves a really social relation? Not the least in the world! Certain sophists, who were called economists, and who were to our sociologists of to-day what the alchemists formerly were to the chemists or the astrologers to the astronomers, had given credit, it is true, to this error—that society essentially consists in an exchange of services. From this point of view, which, moreover, is quite out of date, the social bond could never be closer than that between the ass and the ass driver, the ox and drover, the sheep and the shepherd. Society, we now know, consists in the exchange of reflections. Mutually to ape one another, and by dint of accumulated apings diversely combined to create an originality is the important thing. Reciprocal service is only an accessory. That is why the urban life of former days being principally founded on the organic and natural, rather than on the social relation of producer to consumer, or of workman to employer, was itself only a very imperfect kind of social life, and accordingly the source of endless disagreements.

If it has been possible for us to realise the most perfect and the most intense social life that has ever been seen, it is thanks to the extreme simplicity of our strictly so-called wants. At a time when man was "panivorous" and omnivorous, the craving for food was broken up into an infinity of petty ramifications. To-day it is confined to eating meat which has been preserved in the best of refrigerators. Within the space of an hour each morning, a single member of society by the employment of our ingenious transport machinery feeds a thousand of his kind. The need of clothing has been pretty nearly abolished by the softness of an ever constant climate, and, we must also admit it, by the absence of silkworms and of textile plants. That would perhaps be a disadvantage were it not for the incomparable beauty of our bodies, which lends a real charm to this grand simplicity of costume. Let us observe, however, that it is fairly customary to wear coats of asbestos spangled with mica, of silver interwoven and enriched with gold, in which the refined and delicate charms of our women appear as though moulded in metal, rather than completely screened from view. This metallic iridescence with its infinite tints has a most delightful effect. These are, however, costumes that never wear out. How many clothiers, milliners, tailors, and drapery establishments are thereby abolished at a single stroke! The need of shelter remains, it is true, but it has been greatly reduced. One is no longer obliged to sleep at "starlight-hotel". When a young man grows weary of the life in common which has hitherto sufficed him in the spacious working-drawing-room of his fellows, and desires for matrimonial reasons to have a dwelling to himself, he has only to apply the boring-machine somewhere against the rocky wall and his cell is excavated in a few days. There is no rent and few articles of furniture. The joint-stock furniture, which is magnificent, is almost the only one of which the pair of lovers make use.

The quota of absolute necessities being thus reduced to almost nothing, the quota of superfluities has been able to be extended to almost everything. Since we live on so little, there remains abundant time for thought. A minimum of utilitarian work and a maximum of æsthetic, is surely civilisation itself in its most essential element. The room left vacant in the heart by the reduction of our wants is taken up by the talents—those artistic, poetic, and scientific talents which, as they day by day multiply and take deeper root, become really and truly acquired wants. They really spring, however, from a necessity to produce, and not from a necessity to consume. I underline this difference. The manufacturer is ever toiling, not for his own pleasure nor for that of the world about him, of his fellow-men or his natural rivals, but for a society different from his own—on mutual terms, but that is immaterial. His work, therefore, constitutes a non-social, an almost anti-social relationship with those who are not of his kind, to the great hurt and hindrance of his relations with those who are. The increasing intensity of his work tends to accentuate and not to attenuate the dissimilarities between the different grades of society, which act as an obstacle to the general reunion. We have clearly seen the truth of this in the course of the twentieth century of the ancient era, when the whole population was divided into trades-unions of the different professions, which waged desperate warfare on one another, and whose members in the bosom of each union hated one another as only brothers can.

But for the scientist, the artist, the lover of beauty in all its forms, to produce is a passion, to consume is only a taste. For every artist has a dilettante double. But his dilettantism in respect to arts other than his own only plays by comparison a secondary part in his life. The artist creates through sheer delight, and he alone creates for such motives.

We can now comprehend the depth of the truly social revolution which was accomplished from the days when the æsthetic activity, by dint of ever growing, ended by vanquishing utilitarian activity. Henceforth in place of the relation of producer to consumer has been substituted, as preponderating element in human dealings, the relation of the artist to the art-lover. The ancient social ideal was to seek amusement or self-satisfaction apart and to render mutual service. For this we substitute the following: to be one's own servant and mutually to delight one another. Henceforward, to insist once more, society reposes, not on the exchange of services, but on the exchange of admiration or criticism, of favourable or unfavourable judgments. The anarchical regime of greed in all its forms has been succeeded by the autocratic government of enlightened opinion which has become supreme. For our worthy ancestors deceived themselves finely when they persuaded themselves that social progress led to what they termed freedom of thought. We have something better; we possess the joy and the strength of the mind which attains a certainty of its own, founded, as it is, on its only sure basis, the unanimity of other minds on certain essential matters. On this rock we can rear the highest constructions of thought, nay, the most gigantic systems of philosophy.

The error, at present recognised, of those ancient visionaries called socialists was their failure to see that this life in common, this intense social life, they dreamt of so ardently, had for its indispensable condition the æsthetic life and the universal propagation of the religion of truth and beauty. The latter assumes the drastic lopping off of numerous personal wants. Consequently in rushing, as they did, into an exaggerated development of commercial life, they were marching in the opposite direction to their own goal.

They must have begun, I am well aware, by uprooting the fatal habit of eating bread, which made man a slave to the tyrannical whims of a plant, of beasts which were necessary for the manuring of this plant, and of other plants which served as fodder for their beasts.... But as long as this unhappy craving was rampant and they refrained from combating it, it was obligatory to abstain from arousing others which were not less anti-social, that is to say, not less natural. It was far better to leave men at the ploughtail than to attract them to the factory, for the dispersion and isolation of individualist types are more preferable to bringing them together, which can only result in setting them by the ears. But let us hurry on. All the advantages for which we are indebted to our anti-natural position are now clear. We alone have realised all the quintessence of refinement and reality, of strength and of sweetness, that the social life contains. Formerly, here and there, in a few rare cases in the midst of deserts an individual had certainly had a distant foretaste of this ineffable thing, not to mention three or four salons in the eighteenth century under the ancient regime, two or three painters' studios, one or two green-rooms. They represented, in a way, imperceptible cores of social protoplasm lost amid a mass of foreign matter. But this marrow has become the entire bone at present. Our cities, all in all, are one vast workshop, household and reception hall. And this has happened in the simplest and most inevitable manner in the world. Following the law of separation of the old Herbert Spencer, the selection of heterogeneous talents and vocations was bound to take place of its own accord. In fact, at the end of a century there was already underground in course of development and continuous excavation a city of painters, a city of sculptors, a city of musicians, of poets, of geometricians, of physicists, of chemists, even of naturalists, of psychologists, of scientific or æsthetic specialists of every kind, except, strictly speaking, in philosophy. For we were obliged after several attempts to give up the idea of founding or maintaining a city of philosophers, notably owing to the incessant trouble caused by the tribe of sociologists who are the most unsociable of mankind.

Let us not forget, by the way, to mention the city of "sappers" (we no longer speak of architects), whose speciality is to work out the plans for excavating and repairing all our crypts and to direct the carrying out of the work by our machines. Quitting the hackneyed paths of former architecture, they have created in every detail our modern architecture so profoundly original of which nothing could give an idea to our forefathers. The public building of the ancient architect was a kind of massive and voluminous work of art. It was entirely a thing by itself. Its exterior, and especially its front, occupied his attention far more than the inside. For the modern architect the interior alone exists, and each work is linked on to those which have gone before. None stands by itself. They are only an extension and ramification, one of another, an endless continuation like the epics of the East. The work of the ancient architect with its misplaced individuality, with its symmetry, which gave it a mock air of being a living thing, yet only rendered it more out of keeping with the surrounding landscape, the more symmetrical and more skilfully designed it was, produced the effect of a verse in prose, or of a hackneyed theme in a fantasia. Its special function was to represent correctness, coldness, and stiffness amid the luxuriant disorder of nature and the freedom of the other arts. But to-day, instead of being the most tight-laced of the arts, architecture is the freest and most wanton of them all. It is the chief element of picturesqueness in our life, its artificial and veritably artistic scenery lends to all the masterpieces of our painters and sculptors the horizon of its perspective, the sky of its vaults, the tangled vegetation of its innumerable colonnades, whose shafts are a copy of the idealised trunk of all the antique essence of tree-life, whose capitals imitate the idealised form of all the antique flowers. Here is nature winnowed and perfected, which has become human in order to delight humanity, and which humanity has deified in order to shelter love beneath its shade. This perfection has only been, however, attained after much groping in the dark. Many falls of rock, occasioned by foolhardy excavations, which unduly reduced the number of supports, swallowed up whole towns during the first two centuries. They will serve for our descendants as Pompeii to rediscover. At the least shock produced by earthquakes (the only natural plague which engages our attention), a few cases of crushing to death still occur here and there, but such accidents are very rare.

To return to our subject. Each of our cities in founding colonies in the region round it, has become the mother of cities similar to itself, in which its own peculiar colour has been multiplied in different tints which reflect and render it more beautiful. It is thus with us that nations are formed whose differences no longer correspond to geographical accidents but to the diversity of the social aptitudes of human nature and of nothing else. Nay, more, in each of them the division of cities is founded on that of schools, the most flourishing of which, at any given moment, raises its particular town to the rank of capital, thanks to the all-powerful favour of the public.

The beginnings and devolution of power, questions which have so deeply agitated humanity of yore, arise with us in the most natural way in the world. There is always amid the crowd of our genius, a superior genius who is hailed as such by the almost unanimous acclamation of his pupils at first, and next of his comrades. A man is judged in fact by his peers and according to his productions, not by the incompetent or according to his electoral exploits. In the light of the intimate sense of corporate life which binds and cements us one to another, the elevation of such a dictator to the supreme magistracy has nothing humiliating about it for the pride of the senators who have elected him, and who are the chiefs of all the leading schools they themselves have created. The elector who is a pupil, the elector who is an intelligent and sympathetic admirer identifies himself with the object of his choice. Now it is the particular characteristic of a "Geniocratic" Republic to be based on admiration, not on envy, on sympathy, and not on dislike—on enlightenment, not on illusion.

Nothing is more delightful than a tour through our domains. Our towns, which are quite close to one another are severally connected by broad roads which are always illuminated and dotted with light and graceful monocycles, with trains without smoke or whistle, with pretty electric carriages which glide silently along, like gondolas between walls covered with admirable bas-reliefs, with charming inscriptions, with immortal fancies, the outpourings and accumulations of ten generations of wandering artists. Similarly one might have seen in the olden times the scanty remains of some convent where, in the course of ages the monks had translated their weariness of spirit into grinning figures, with hooded heads, into beasts from the Apocalypse, clumsily sculptured on the capitals of the little pilasters or around the stone chair of the Abbot. But what a distance lies between this monkish nightmare and this artistic revelation! At the very most the pretty little gallery which joined across the Arno, the museum of the Pitti Palace, with that of the Uffizi at Florence, could give our ancestors a faint idea of what we see.

If the corridors of our abode possess this wealth and splendour, what shall we say of the dwelling-places, or of the cities? They are filled with heaps of artistic marvels, of frescoes, enamels, gold and silver plate, bronzes and pictures, the acme and quintessence of musical emotions, of philosophic conceptions, of poetic dreams, enough to baffle all description, and weary all admiration. We have difficulty in believing that the labyrinth of galleries, subterranean palaces and marble catacombs, all named and numbered, whose manifold nomenclature recalls all the geography and history of the past, have been excavated in so few centuries. That is what perseverance can do! However accustomed we may be to this extraordinary sight, it still at times happens when wandering alone, during the hours of the siesta, in this sort of infinite cathedral, with its irregular and endless architecture, through this forest of lofty columns, massive or in close formation, displaying in turn the most diversified and grandiose styles, Egyptian, Greek, Byzantine, Arab, Gothic, and reminiscent of all the vanished and venerated floras and faunas, when it is not above all profoundly original ... it happens, I repeat, that panting, and beside ourselves with ecstasy, we come to a standstill, like the traveller of yore when he entered the twilight of a virgin forest, or of the pillared hall of Karnak.

To those who on reading the ancient accounts of travels might perchance have regretted the wanderings of caravans across the deserts or the discoveries of new worlds, our universe can offer boundless excursions under the Atlantic and Pacific Oceans frozen to their very lowest depths. Venturesome explorers, I was going to say discoverers, have in every direction and in the easiest imaginable fashion honeycombed these immense ice-caps with endless passages much in the same way as the termites, according to our palæontologists, bored through the floors of our fathers. We extend at will these fantastic galleries of crystal, which, wherever they cross one another, form so many crystal palaces, by casting on the walls a ray of intense heat which makes them melt. We take good care to drain the water due to the liquefaction into one of those bottomless pits which here and there yawn hideously beneath our feet. Thanks to this method and the improvements it has undergone we have succeeded in cutting, hewing and carving the solidified sea-water. We are able to glide through it, to manoeuvre in it, to course through it on skates or velocipedes with an ease and agility that are always admired in spite of our being accustomed to it. The severe cold of these regions is scarcely tempered by millions of electric lamps which are mirrored in these emerald-green icicles with their velvet-like tints and renders a permanent stay impossible. It would even prevent us crossing them if, by good luck, the earliest pioneers had not discovered in them crowds of seals which had been caught while still alive by the freezing of the waters in which they remain imprisoned. Their carefully prepared skins have furnished us with warm clothing. Nothing is more curious than thus suddenly to catch sight of, as it were through a mysterious glass case, one of these huge marine animals, sometimes a whale, a shark or a devil fish, and that star-like flora which carpets the seas. Though appearing crystallized in its transparent prison, in its Elysium of pure brine, it has lost none of its secret charm, that was quite unknown to our ancestors. Idealised by its very lack of motion, immortalised by its death, it dimly shines here and there with gleams of pearl and mother of pearl in the twilight of the depths below, to the right, the left, beneath the feet or above the head of the solitary skater who roams with his lamp on his forehead in pursuit of the unknown. There is always something new to look forward to from these miraculous soundings, so different from the soundings of former time. Never a tourist has come home without having discovered some interesting object—a piece of wreckage, the steeple of some sunken town, a human skeleton to enrich our prehistoric museums, sometimes a shoal of sardines or cod. These splendid and timely reserves come in very handy for replenishing our bill of fare. But the chief fascination of such adventurous exploration is the sense of the boundless and the everlasting, of the unfathomable and the changeless by which one is arrested and overwhelmed in these bottomless depths. The savour of this silence and solitude, of this profound peace, the sequel to so many tempests, of this almost starless gloaming and twilight with its fleeting gleams, reposes the eye after our underground illuminations. I will not speak of the surprises which the hand of man has lavished there. At the moment when one least expects it one sees the submarine tunnel along which one is gliding, enlarged beyond all measure and transformed into a vast hall in which the fancy of our sculptors has found full play, a temple of vast dimensions with transparent pillars, with walls of enthralling beauty that the eye in ecstasy attempts to fathom. That is often the trysting place of friends and lovers, and the excursion begun in dreamy loneliness is continued in loving companionship.

But we have wandered long enough in these halls of mysteries. Let us return to our cities. One would look, by the bye, in vain for a city of lawyers there, or even, for a court of justice. There is no more arable land and therefore no more lawsuits about property or ancient rights. There are no more walls, and therefore no more lawsuits about party walls. As for felonies and misdemeanours, we do not know exactly why, but it is an obvious fact that with the spread of the cult of art they have disappeared as by enchantment, while formerly the progress of industrial life had tripled their numbers in half a century.

Man in becoming a town dweller has become really human. From the time that all sorts of trees and beasts, of flowers and insects no longer interpose between men, and all sorts of vulgar wants no longer hinder the progress of the truly human faculties, every one seems to be born well-bred, just as every one is born a sculptor or musician, philosopher or poet, and speaks the most correct language with the purest accent. An indescribable courtesy, skilled to charm without falsehood, to please without obsequiousness, the most free from fawning one has ever seen, is united to a politeness which has at heart the feeling, not of a social hierarchy to be respected, but of a social harmony to be maintained. It is composed not of more or less degenerate airs of the court, but of more or less faithful reflections of the heart. Its refinement is such as the race who lived on the surface of earth never even dreamed of. It permeates like a fragrant oil all the complicated and delicate machinery of our existence. No unsociableness, no misanthropy can resist it. The charm is too profound. The single threat of ostracism, I do not say of expulsion to the realms above, which would be a death sentence, but of banishment beyond the limits of the usual corporate life, is sufficient to arrest the most criminal natures on the slope of crime. There is in the slightest inflexion of voice, in the least inclination of the head of our women a special charm, which is not only the charm of former times, whether roguish kindness or kindly roguishness, but a refinement at once more exquisite and more healthful in which the constant practice of seeing and doing beautiful things or loving and being loved is expressed in an ineffable fashion.

VI.
LOVE

Love, in fact, is the unseen and perennial source of this novel courtesy. The capital importance it has assumed, the strange forms it has worn, the unexpected heights to which it has risen, are perhaps the most significant characteristics of our civilisation. In the glittering and superficial epochs, age of paper and electro-plating, which immediately preceded our present era, love was held in check by a thousand childish needs, by the contagious mono-mania of unsightly and cumbersome luxury or of ceaseless globe-trotting, and by that other form of madness which has now disappeared, the so-called political ambition. It suffered accordingly an immense decline, relatively speaking. To-day it benefits from the destruction or gradual diminution of all the other principal impulses of the heart which have taken refuge and concentrated themselves in it as banished mankind has done in the warm bosom of the earth. Patriotism is dead, since there is no longer any native land, but only a native grot. Moreover the guilds which we enter as we please according to our vocations have taken the place of Fatherlands. Corporate spirit has exterminated patriotism. In the same fashion the school is on the road not to exterminate but to transform the family, which is only right and proper. The best that can be said for the parents of old was that they were compulsory and not always cost-free friends. One was not wrong in preferring in general to them friends who are a species of optional and unselfish relations. Maternal love itself has undergone a good many transformations among our women artists, and one must admit, sundry partial set backs.

But love is left to us. Or rather, be it said without vanity, it is we who discovered and introduced it. Its name has preceded it by a good many centuries. Our ancestors gave it its name, but they spoke of it as the Hebrews spoke of the Messiah. It has revealed itself in our day. In our day it has become incarnate, it has founded the true religion, universal and enduring, that pure and austere moral which is indistinguishable from art. It has been favoured at the outset, beyond all doubt and beyond all expectation by the charm and beauty of our women, who are all differently yet almost equally accomplished. There is nothing *natural* left in our world below if it be not they. But it appears they have always been the most beautiful thing in nature even in the most unfavourable and ill-favoured ages. For we are assured that never was the graceful curve of hill or stream, of wave or rippling cornfield, that never was the hue of the dawn or of the Mediterranean equal in sweetness, in strength, in richness of visible music and harmony to the female form. There must therefore have been a special instinct which is quite incomprehensible which formerly retained the poor beside their natal river or rock and prevented their emigrating to the big towns, where they might well have hoped to admire at their ease tints and outlines of beauty assuredly far superior to the charm of the locality to whose attractions they fell a victim. At present there is no other country than the woman of one's affections; there is no other home-sickness than that caused by her absence.

But the foregoing is insufficient to explain the unparalleled power and persistence of our love which time intensifies more than it wears out, and consummates as it consumes it. Love, we now at last know, is like air, essential to life; we must look to it for health and not for mere nourishment. It is as the sun once was, we must use it to give us light, not allow it to dazzle us. It resembles that imposing temple that the fervour of our fathers raised in its honour when they worshipped it, unwittingly, at the Paris Opera-house. The most beautiful part of it is the staircase—when one mounts it. We have therefore attempted to make the staircase monopolise the whole edifice without leaving the tiniest room for the hall. The wise man, an ancient writer has said, is to the woman what the asymptote is to the curve, it draws ever nearer but never touches. It was a half crazy fellow named Rousseau who uttered this splendid aphorism and our society flatters itself that it has practised it far better than he. All the same the ideal thus outlined, we are compelled to confess, is rarely attained in all its entity. This degree of perfection is reserved for the most saintly souls, the ascetics, men and women, who wander together, two and two, in the most marvellous cloisters, in the most Raphaelesque cells in the city of painters, in a sort of artificial dusk produced by a coloured twilight in the midst of a throng of similar couples, and on the banks of a stream so to say of audacious and splendid revelations of the nude. They pass their life in feasting their eyes on these waves of beauty, the living bank of which is their own passion. Together they climb the fiery steps of the heavenly staircase to the very summit on which they halt. Then supremely inspired they set to work and produce masterpieces. Heroic lovers are they whose whole pleasure in love consists in the sublime joy of feeling their love growing within them, blissful because it is shared, inspiring because it is chaste.

But for the greater number of us it has been necessary to come down to the level of the insurmountable weakness of the old Adam. None the less the inelastic limits of our food supplies have made it a duty for us rigorously to guard against a possible excess in our population which has reached to-day fifty millions, a figure it can never exceed without danger. We have been obliged to forbid in general under the most severe penalties a practice which apparently was very common and indulged in *ad libitum* by our forefathers. Is it possible that after manufacturing the rubbish heaps of law with which our libraries are lumbered up, they precisely omitted to regulate the only matter considered worthy to-day of regulation? Can we conceive that it could ever have been permissible to the first comer without due authorisation to expose society to the arrival of a new hungry and wailing member—above all at a time when it was not possible to kill a partridge without a game licence, or to import a sack of corn without paying duty? Wiser and more far-sighted, we degrade, and in case of a second offence we condemn to be thrown into a lake of petroleum, whoever allows himself to infringe our constitutional law on this point, or rather we should say, should allow himself, for the force of public opinion has got the better of the crime and has rendered our penalties unnecessary. We sometimes, nay very often, see lovers who go mad from love and die in consequence. Others courageously get themselves hoisted by a lift to the gaping mouth of an extinct volcano and reach the outer air which in a moment freezes them to death. They have scarcely time to regard the azure sky—a magnificent spectacle, so they say—and the twilight hues of the still dying sun or the vast and unstudied disorder of the stars; then locked in each other's arms they fall dead upon the ice! The summit of their favourite volcano is completely crowned with their corpses which are admirably preserved always in twos, stark and livid, a living image still of love and agony, of despair and frenzy, but more often of ecstatic repose. They recently made an indelible impression on a celebrated traveller who was bold enough to make the ascent in order to get a glimpse of them. We all know how he has since died from the effects.

But what is unheard of and unexampled in our day is for a woman in love to abandon herself to her lover before the latter has under her inspiration produced a masterpiece which is adjudged and proclaimed as such by his rivals. For here we have the indispensable condition to which legitimate marriage is subordinated. The right to have children is the monopoly and supreme recompense of genius. It is besides a powerful lever for the uplifting and exaltation of the race. Futhermore a man can only exercise it exactly the same number of times as he produces works worthy of a master. But in this respect some indulgence is shown. It even happens pretty frequently that touched by pity for some grand passion that disposes only of a mediocre talent, the affected admiration of the public partly from sympathy and partly from condescension accords a favourable verdict to works of no intrinsic value. Perhaps there are also (in fact there is no doubt about it) for common use other methods of getting round the law.

Ancient society reposed on the fear of punishment, on a penal system which has had its day. Ours, it is clear, is based on the expectation of happiness. The enthusiasm and creative fire aroused by such a perspective are attested by our exhibitions, and borne witness to by the rich luxuriance of our annual art harvests. When we think of the precisely opposite effects of ancient marriage, that institution of our ancestors, more ridiculous still than their umbrellas, one can measure the distance between this excessive and pretended exclusive *debitum conjugale* and our mode of union, at once free and regulated, energetic and intermittent, passionate and restrained, the true corner-stone of our regenerated humanity. The sufferings it imposes on those who are sacrificed, the unsuccessful artists, is not for the latter a cause of complaint. Their despair itself is dear to the desperate; for if they do not die of it, they draw life and immortality from it and from the bottomless pit of their inner depth of woe, they gather deathless flowers, flowers of art or poesy for some, mystic roses for others. To the latter perhaps is given at that moment, as they grope in their inward darkness to touch most nearly the essence of things, and these delights are so vivid that our artists and our metaphysical mystics wonder whether art and philosophy were made to console love or if the sole reason for love's existence is not to inspire art and the pursuit of ultimate truth. This last opinion has generally prevailed.

The extent to which love has refined our habits, and to which our civilisation based on love is superior in morality to the former civilisation based on ambition and covetousness, was proved at the time of the great discovery which took place in the Year of Salvation 194. Guided by some mysterious inkling, some electric sense of direction, a bold sapper by dint of forcing his way through the flanks of the earth beyond the ordinary galleries suddenly penetrated into a strange open space buzzing with human voices and swarming with human faces. But what squeaky voices! What sallow complexions! What an impossible language with no connection with our Greek! It was, without doubt, a veritable underground America, quite as vast and still more curious. It was the work of a little tribe of burrowing Chinese who had had, one imagines, the same idea as our Miltiades. Much more practical than he, they had hastily crawled underground without encumbering themselves with museums and libraries, and there they had multiplied enormously. Instead of confining themselves as we to turning to account the deposits of animal carcasses, they had shamelessly given themselves up to ancestral cannibalism. They were thus enabled, seeing the thousand of millions of Chinese destroyed and buried beneath the snow, to give full vent to their prolific instincts. Alas! who knows if our own descendants will not one day be reduced to this extremity? In what promiscuity, in what a slough of greed, falsehood and robbery were these unfortunates living! The words of our language refuse to depict their filth and coarseness. With infinite pains they raised underground diminutive vegetables in diminutive beds of soil they had brought thither together with diminutive pigs and dogs.... These ancient servants of mankind appeared very disgusting to our new Christopher Columbus. These degraded beings (I speak of the masters and not of the animals, for the latter belong to a breed that has been much improved by those who raised them) had lost all recollection of the Middle Empire and even of the surface of the earth. They heartily laughed when some of our *savants* sent on a mission to them spoke to them of the firmament, the sun, the moon and the stars.... They listened, however, to the end of these accounts, then in an ironical tone they asked our envoys: «Have you seen all that?" And the latter unfortunately could not reply to the question, since no one among us has seen the sky except the lovers who go to die together.

Now, what did our settlers do at the sight of such cerebral atrophy? Several proposed, it is true, to exterminate these savages who might well become dangerous owing to their cunning and to their numbers, and to appropriate their dwelling-place after a certain amount of cleaning and painting and the removal of numerous little bells. Others proposed to reduce them to the status of slaves or servants in order to shift on to them all our menial work. But these two proposals were rejected. An attempt was made to civilize and to render less savage these poor cousins, and once the impossibility of any success in that direction had been ascertained the partition was carefully blocked up.

VII.
THE ÆSTHETIC LIFE

Such is the moral miracle wrought by our excellence which itself is begotten of love and beauty. But the intellectual marvels which have issued from the same source, merit a still more extended notice. It will be enough for me to indicate them as I go along.

Let us first speak of the sciences. One might have thought that from the day that the stars and celestial bodies, the faunas and floras, ceased to play a certain part in our lives or that the manifold sources of observation and experience ceased to flow, astronomy and meteorology would henceforth be brought to a standstill while zoology and botany would have become palæontology pure and simple, without speaking of their application to the navy, army and agriculture, which are all to-day entirely obsolete; in fact, that they would have ceased to make a step forward and would have fallen into complete oblivion. Luckily these apprehensions proved groundless. Let us admire the extent to which the sciences which the past has bequeathed to us, formerly eminently useful and inductive, have for the first time had the advantage of passionately interesting and exciting the general public since they have acquired this double characteristic of being an object of luxury and a deductive subject. The past has accumulated such undigested masses of astronomical tables, papers and proceedings dealing with measurements, vivisections, and innumerable experiments, that the human mind can live on this capital till the end of time. It was high time that it began at last to arrange and utilize these materials. Now, for the sciences of which I am speaking, the advantage is great from the point of view of their success that they are entirely based on written testimony, and in no way on sense perception, and that they on all occasions invoke the authority of books (for we talk to-day of whole bibliographies when formerly people spoke of a single Bible—evidently an immense difference). This great and inestimable advantage consists in the extraordinary riches of our libraries in documents of the most diverse kinds which never leaves an ingenious theorist in the lurch, and is equal to supporting in a plenary and authoritative fashion the most contradictory opinions at one and the same symposium. Its abundance recalls the admirable wealth of antique legislation and jurisprudence in texts and decisions of every hue which rendered the lawsuits so interesting, almost as much as the battles of the populace of Alexandria on the subject of a theological iota. The debates of our *savants*, their polemics relative to the Vitellin yolk of the egg of the Arachneida, or the digestive apparatus of the Infusoria, constitute the burning questions which distress us, and which if we had the misfortune to possess a regular press, would not fail to drench our streets in gore. For the questions which are useless and even harmful have always the knack of rousing the passions, provided they are insoluble.

These are our religious quarrels. In fact the sum total of the sciences bequeathed to us by the past has become definitely and inevitably a religion. Our *savants* to-day who work deductively on these data from henceforth changeless and inviolate, exactly recall on a much larger scale the theologians of the ancient world. This new encyclopædic theology, not less fertile than others in schisms and heresies, is the unique but inexhaustible source of divisions in the bosom of our Church which is otherwise so compact. It is perhaps the most profound and fascinating charm of our intellectual leaders.

"All the same, they are dead sciences!" say certain malcontents. Let us accept the epithet. They are dead, if one likes, but after the fashion of those languages in which a whole people chanted its hymns although no one speaks them any longer. This is also the case with certain faces whose beauty only appears in its fulness when their last sleep has come. Let none therefore be surprised if our love fastens on these majestic dogmas, by which we are more and more overshadowed, on these higher inutilities which are our vocation. Above all, mathematics, as being the most perfect type of the new sciences, has progressed with giant steps. Descending to fabulous depths, analysis has allowed the astronomers at length to attack and to solve problems whose mere statement would have provoked an incredulous smile in their predecessors. And so they discover every day, chalk in hand, not with the telescope to the eye, I know not how many intra-mercurial or extra-neptunian planets, and begin to distinguish the planets of the nearer stars. There are in this department, in the comparative anatomy and physiology of numerous solar systems, the most novel and profound views. Our Leverriers are reckoned by hundreds. Being all the better acquainted with the sky because they no longer see it, they resemble Beethoven, who only wrote his finest symphonies when he had lost his hearing. Our Claude Bernards and Pasteurs are almost as numerous. Although we are careful as a matter of fact not to accord to the natural sciences the exaggerated and fundamentally anti-social importance they formerly usurped during two or three centuries, we do not completely neglect them. Even the applied sciences have their votaries. Recently one of the latter has at last discovered—such is the irony of destiny—the practical means of steering balloons. These discoveries are useless, I admit, yet are ever beautiful and fertile, fertile in new, if superfluous, beauties. They are welcomed with transports of feverish enthusiasm and win for their originators something better than glory,—the happiness that we know so well.

But among the sciences there are two which are still experimental and inductive and in addition pre-eminently useful. It is to this exceptional standing that they perhaps owe, we must admit, the unparalled rapidity with which they have grown. These two sciences which were formerly the antipodes of one another, are to-day on the high road to becoming identical by dint of pushing their joint researches ever deeper and crushing to atoms the last problems left. Their names are chemistry and psychology.

Our chemists, inspired perhaps by love and better instructed in the nature of affinities, force their way into the inner life of the molecules and reveal to us their desires, their ideas, and under a fallacious air of conformity, their individual physiognomy. While they thus construct for us the psychology of the atom, our psychologists explain to us the atomic theory of self, I was going to say the sociology of self. They enable us to perceive, even in its most minute detail, the most admirable of all societies, this hierarchy of consciousness, this feudal system of vassal souls, of which our personality is the summit. We are indebted to them both for priceless benefits. Thanks to the former we are no longer alone in a frozen world. We are conscious that these rocks are alive and animated, we are conscious that these hard metals which protect and warm us are likewise a prolific brotherhood. Through their mediation these living stones have some message for our heart, something at once alien and intimate, which neither the stars nor the flowers of the field ever told to our forefathers. And by their mediation also, and the service is not to be despised—we have learnt certain processes which allow us (in a scanty measure, it is true, for the moment) to supplement the insufficiency of our ordinary food supplies, or to vary their monotony by several substances agreeable to the taste and entirely compounded by artificial means. But if our chemists have thus reassured us against the danger of dying of hunger, our psychologists have acquired still further claims on our gratitude in freeing us from the fear of death. Permeated by their doctrines we have followed their consequences to their final conclusion with the deductive vigour that is second nature with us. Death appears to us as a dethronement that leads to freedom. It restores to itself the fallen or abdicated self that retires anew into its inner consciousness, where it finds in depths more than the equivalent of the outward empire it has lost. In thinking of the terrors of former man, face to face with the tomb, we compare them with the dread experienced by the comrades of Miltiades when they were compelled to bid adieu to the fields of ice, to the snowy horizons, in order to enter for ever the gloomy abysses in which such a myriad of glittering and marvellous surprises awaited them.

That is a well-established doctrine and one on which no discussion would be tolerated. It is, with our devotion to beauty and our faith in the divine omnipotence of love, the foundation of our peace of mind and the starting point of our enthusiasms. Our philosophers themselves avoid touching on it, as on all which is fundamental in our institutions. To this perhaps may be traced an agreeable air of harmlessness which adds to the charm of their refinement and contributes to their success in public. With such certainties as ballast we can spring with a light heart into the æther of systems, and so we do not fail to do so. One may be surprised, however, that I made a distinction between our philosophers and those deductive *savants* of whom I have spoken above. Their subject-matter and their methods are identical. They chew the cud—if I may be allowed the expression—in the same fashion at the same mangers. But the one group, I mean the *savants*, are ordinary ruminants, that is, slow and clumsy. The others have the peculiar quality of being at once ruminants and nimble, like the antelope. And this difference of temperament is indelible.

There is not, I have already said, a city, but there is a grotto of philosophers, a natural one to which they come, and sit apart from one another or in groups, according to their schools, on chairs formed of granite blocks beside a petrifying well. This spacious grotto contains astounding stalactites, the slow product of continuous droppings which vaguely imitate, in the eyes of those who are not too critical, all kinds of beautiful objects, cups and chandeliers, cathedrals and mirrors—cups which quench no man's thirst, chandeliers which give no light, cathedrals in which no one prays, but mirrors in which one sees oneself more or less faithfully and pleasantly portrayed. There also is to be seen a gloomy and bottomless lake over which hang like so many question-marks, the pendants in the sombre roof and the beards of the thinkers. Such is the ample cave which is exactly identical to the philosophy it shelters, with its crystals sparkling amid its uncertain shadows—full of precipices, it is true. It recalls better than anything else to the new race of men, but with a still greater portion of mirage-like fascination, that diurnal miracle of our forefathers—the starry night. Now the crowd of systematic ideas which slowly form and crystallise there in each brain like mental stalactites is indescribably enormous. While all the former stalactites of thought are for ever ramifying and changing their shape, turning as it were from a table into an altar, or from an eagle into a griffin, new ideas appear here and there still more surprising. There are always, of course, Neo-Aristotelians, Neo-Kantians, Neo-Cartesians, and Neo-Pythagoricians. Let us not forget the commentators of Empedocles to whom his passion for the volcanic underworld has procured an unexpected rejuvenation of his antique authority on the minds of men, above all since an archæologist has maintained he has found the skeleton of this grand man in pushing an exploring gallery to the very foot of Ætna which to-day is completely extinct. But there is ever arising some great reformer with an unpublished gospel that each attempts to enrich with a new version destined to take its place. I will cite for example the greatest intellect of our time, the chief of the fashionable school in sociology. According to this profound thinker the social development of humanity, starting on the outer rind of the earth and continuing to-day beneath its crust, at no great distance from the surface, is destined in proportion to the growing solar and planetary cooling, to pursue its course from strata to strata down to the very centre of the earth, while the population forcibly contracts and civilisation on the contrary expands at each new descent. It is worth seeing the vigour and Dante-like precision with which he characterises the social type peculiar to each of these humanities, immured within its own circle, growing ever nobler and richer, happier and better balanced. One should read the portrait which he has limned with a bold brush of the last man, sole survivor and heir of a hundred successive civilisations, left to himself yet self-sufficient in the midst of his immense stores of science and art. He is happy as a god because he is omniscient and omnipotent, because he has just discovered the true answer of the Great Enigma, yet dying because he cannot survive humanity. By means of an explosive substance of extraordinary potency he blows up the globe with himself in order to sow the immensity of space with the last remnants of mankind. This system very naturally has a good many adherents. The graceful Hypatias, however, who form his female followers, idly lying round the master's stone, are agreed it would be proper to associate with the last man, the last woman, not less ideal than he.

But what shall I say of art and poetry? Here to be just, praise must become panegyric. Let us limit ourselves to indicating the general tendency of the transformations that have taken place. I have related what has become of our architecture which has been turned "outside in", so to say, and brought into keeping with its surroundings, the idealised image in stone, the essence and consummation of former Nature. I shall not return to the subject. But I must still say a word about this immortal and overflowing population of statues, this wealth of frescoes, enamels, and bronzes which in concert with our poetry celebrate in this architectural transfiguration of the nether world the apotheosis of love. There would be an interesting study to make on the gradual metamorphoses that the genius of our painters and sculptors has imposed for the last three centuries on these traditional types of lions, horses, tigers, birds, trees and flowers, with which it is never weary of disporting itself, without being either helped or hindered by the sight of any animal or any plant. Never, in fact, have our artists, who protest strongly against being taken for photographers, depicted so many plants, animals and landscapes, than since these were no more. Similarly, they have never painted or sculptured so many draperies, since everyone goes about almost naked, while formerly at the time when humanity wore clothes the nude abounded in art. Does it mean that nature, now dead and formerly alive, from which our great masters drew their subjects and themes, has become a simple hieroglyphic and coldly conventional alphabet? No. Daughter to-day of tradition and no longer of productive nature, humanised and harmonised, she has a still firmer hold on the heart. If she recalls to each his day-dreams rather than his recollections, his imaginings rather than his impressions, his admiration as an artist rather than his terror as a child, she is only the better calculated to fascinate and subdue. She has for us the profound and intimate charm of an old legend, but it is a legend in which one believes.

Nothing is more inspiring. Such must have been the mythology of the worthy Homer when his hearers in the Cyclades still believed in Aphrodite and Pallas, in the Dioscuri and the Centaurs, of whom he spoke to them and wrung from them tears of sheer delight. Thus our poets make us weep, when they speak to us now of azure skies, of the sea-girt horizon, of the perfume of roses, of the song of birds, of all those objects that our eye has never seen, our ear has never heard, of which all our senses are ignorant, yet our mind conjures them up within us by a strange instinct at the least suggestion of love.

And when our painters show us these horses whose legs grow ever slimmer, these swans whose necks become ever rounder and longer, these vines whose leaves and branches grow ever more intricate with their lace-like edges and arabesques interwoven round still more exquisite birds, a matchless emotion rises within us such as a young Greek might have felt before a bas-relief crowded with fauns and nymphs or with Argonautes bearing off the Golden Fleece, or with Nereids sporting around the cup of Amphitrite.

If our architecture in spite of all its splendours seems but a simple foil of our other fine arts, they in their turn, however admirable, have the air of being barely worthy to illustrate our poetry and literature graven on stone. But in our poetry and even in our literature there are glories which in comparison with less obvious beauty are as the corona is to the ovary, or the frame to the picture. Read our romantic dramas and epics in which all ancient history is magically unrolled down to the heroic struggle and love story of Miltiades. You will decide that nothing more sublime could ever be written. Read also our idylls, our elegies, our epigrams inspired by antiquity, and our poetry of every kind written in a dozen dead languages which when desired revive in order to vivify with their clear notes and their manifold harmonies, the pleasure of our ear, to accompany, so to say, with their rich orchestration in English, German, Swedish, Arabic, Italian and French, the music of our pure Attic. You will imagine nothing more fascinating than this renaissance and transfiguration of forgotten idioms, once the glory of antiquity. As for our dramas and our poems which are often at once the collective and individual work of a school, incarnate in its chief and animated with a single idea like the sculptures of the Parthenon, there is nothing comparable in the masterpieces of Sophocles or Homer. What the extinct species of nature formerly alive are to our painters and sculptors, the no less extinct sentiments of former human nature are to our dramatists. Jealousy, ambition, patriotism, fanaticism, the mad lust of battle, the exalted love of family, the pride of an illustrious name, all the vanished passions of the heart when called up upon the stage, no longer cause tears or terror in a single soul, any more than the heraldic tigers and lions painted up on our public squares frighten our children. But in a new accent with quite a different ring, they speak to us their ancient language; and to tell the truth, they are only a grand piano on which our new passions play. Now there is but a single passion for all its thousand names, as there is above but a single sun. It is love, the soul of our soul and source of our art. That is the true sun which will never fail us, which is never weary of touching and reanimating with the light of its countenance its lower creations of yore, the first-born incarnations of the heart, in order to make them young once more, in order to re-gild them with its dawns, and reincarnadine them with its setting splendours; almost in the same fashion as it sufficed the other sun to compass with a single ray that august summons to deck the earth, addressed to every ancient plant of the field, awakening it to bloom anew, that grand yearly transformation scene, so deceptive and entrancing, which they named the Spring, when there was still a Spring to name!

And so for our highly refined writers, all that I have just praised a moment ago has no value if their heart is left untouched. They would give for one true and personal note all these feats of skill and sleight of hand. What they look for under the most grandiose conceptions and stage effects, and under the most audacious novelties in rhyme; what they adore on bended knee when they have found it, is a short passage, a line, half a line, on which an imperceptible hint of profound passion, or the most fleeting phase, though unexpressed, of love in joy, in suffering or in death has left its impress. Thus at the beginning of humanity each tint of the dawn or the dusk, each hour of the day was, for the first man who gave it a name, a new solar god who soon possessed worshippers, priests and temples of his own. But to analyse sensations after the manner of the old-fashioned erotic writers gives us no trouble. The real difficulty and merit lie in gathering along with our mystics, from the lowest depths of sorrow, its flowers of ecstasy, the pearls and coral that lie at the bottom of its sea, and to enrich the soul in its own eyes. Our purest poetry thus joins hands with our most profound psychology. One is the oracle, the other the dogma of one and the same religion.

And yet is it credible? In spite of its beauty, harmony and incomparable charm, our society has also its malcontents. There are here and there certain recusants who declare they are soaked and saturated with the essence, so remarkably pure and so much above proof, of our excessive and compulsory society. They find our realm of beauty too static, our atmosphere of happiness too tranquil. In vain to please them we vary from time to time the intensity and colouring of our illuminations and ventilate our colonnades with a kind of refreshing breeze. They persist in condemning as monotonous our day devoid of clouds or night; our year, devoid of seasons; our towns devoid of country-life. Very curiously when the month of May comes round, this feeling of restlessness which they alone experience at ordinary times, becomes contagious and well-nigh general. And so it is the most melancholy and least busy month of the year. One would say that the Spring driven from every place, from the gloomy immensity of the heavens and from the frozen surface of the earth has, as we, sought refuge under ground; or rather that her wandering ghost returns at stated seasons to visit us and tantalise us by her haunting presence. It is then that the city of the musicians grows full and their music becomes so sweet, pathetic, mournful, and desperately harrowing that we see lovers by hundreds at a time take each other by the hand and go up to gaze upon the death-dealing sky.... In reference to this I ought to say that there was recently a false alarm caused by a madman who pretended he had seen the sun coming back to life and melting the ice. At this news which had not been otherwise confirmed, quite a considerable portion of the population became unsettled and gave itself up to the pleasing task of forming plans for an early exodus. Such unhealthy and revolutionary dreams evidently only serve to foment artificial discontent.

Luckily a scholar in rummaging in a forgotten corner of the archives put his hand on a big collection of phonographic and cinematographic records which had been amassed by an ancient collector. Interpreted by the phonograph and cinematograph together, these cylinders and films have enabled us suddenly to hear all the former sounds in nature accompanied by their corresponding sights, the thunder, the winds, the mountain torrents, the murmurs that accompany the dawn, the monotonous cry of the osprey and the long drawn out lament of the nightingale amid the manifold whisperings of night. At this resurrection of another age to the ear and eye, of extinct species and vanished phenomena, an immense astonishment quickly followed by an immense disillusion arose among the most ardent partisans of a return to the ancient regime. For that was not what one had hitherto believed on the strength of what even the most realist poets and novelists had told us. It was something infinitely less ravishing and less worthy of our regret. The song of the nightingale above all provoked a most unpleasant surprise. We were all angry with it for showing itself so inferior to its reputation. Assuredly the worst of our concerts is more musical than this so-called symphony of nature with full orchestral accompaniment.

Thus has been quelled by an ingenious expedient entirely unknown to former governments, this first and only attempt at rebellion. May it be the last. A certain leaven of discord is beginning, alas, to contaminate our ranks, and our moralists observe not without apprehension sundry symptoms which indicate the relaxation of our morals. The growth in our population is very disquieting, notably since certain chemical discoveries, following upon which we have been too much in a hurry to declare that bread might be made of stones, and that it was no longer worth while to husband our food supplies or to trouble ourselves to maintain at a certain limit the number of mouths to feed.

Simultaneously with the increase in the number of children, there is a diminution in the number of masterpieces. Let us hope that this lamentable movement will soon abate. If the sun once more, as after the different glacial epochs, succeeds in awakening from his lethargy and regains fresh strength, let us pray that only a small part of our population, that which is the most light-headed, the most unruly, and the most deeply attacked by incurable "matrimonialitis", will avail itself of the seeming yet deceptive advantages offered by this open air cure and will make a dash upwards for the freedom of those inclement climes! But this is highly improbable if one reflects on the advanced age of the sun and the danger of those relapses common to old age. It is still less desirable. Let us repeat in the words of Miltiades our august ancestor, blessed are those stars which are extinct, that is to say, the almost entire number of those which people space. Radiance, as he truly said, is to the stars what the flowering season is to the plants. After having flowered, they begin to bear fruit. Thus, doubtless, weary of expansion and the useless squandering of their strength through the infinite void, the stars collect the germs of higher life in order to fertilize them in the depth of their bosom. The deceptive brilliancy of these widely scattered stars, so relatively few in number, which are still alight, which have not finished sowing what Miltiades called their wild oats of light and heat, prevented the first race of men from thinking of this, to wit of the numberless and tranquil multitude of dark stars to whom this radiance served as a cloak. But as for us, delivered from their spell and freed from this immemorial optical delusion, we continue firmly to believe that, among the stars as among mankind, the most brilliant are not the best, and that the same causes have brought about elsewhere the same results, compelling other races of men to hide themselves in the bosom of their earth, and there in peace to pursue the happy course of their destiny under unique conditions of absolute independence and purity, that in short in the heavens as on the earth true happiness lives concealed.